MEET

Roger L. Simon was born in 1943 in New York City and educated at Dartmouth and Yale. He is best known for his Moses Wine private investigator novels *The Big Fix*, *Wild Turkey*, *Peking Duck*, *California Roll*, *Raising the Dead*, and *The Straight Man*. *The Big Fix* won awards from the Mystery Writers of America and the Crime Writers of Great Britain as the best novel of the year, and it was made into a film. Roger Simon is also a screenwriter and filmmaker, as well as a member of the executive committee of the International Association of Crime Writers. He lives in Los Angeles.

DEAD MEET

ROGER L. SIMON

Black Lizard Books

Berkeley • 1988

Original title: *Heir*

ISBN 0-88739-095-1
Library of Congress Catalog Card No. 87-73466

Manufactured in the United States of America

The Journal

First Day...

I have turned the air conditioner up to high. At first I tried medium-cool, but that didn't work, so I turned the knob all the way to the left. Freezing air rushed out of the vent full force. The temperature outside must have been in the middle thirties, on the cool side for the end of April. Then I crossed the room and turned off the thermostatic control, because this building has enough heat to vitiate my efforts in a matter of minutes. The temperature in the apartment is falling rapidly and now, as I first set my pen to paper, the thermometer reads sixty-three degrees Fahrenheit. I have put on a thin sweater left over from my college days. Actually, it is pretty comfortable. I should leave the apartment at this level all the time. It makes me feel extremely vigorous, and, I must confess, for a man, or, as they say, a youth, of twenty-four, I have always been on the lethargic side. But since six-thirty this evening, about an hour ago, I have been moving with a clear sense of purpose.

I live on the New Jersey side of the Hudson River. Originally, I had one of the two bedroom suites with balconies overlooking the Manhattan skyline, Grant's Tomb and all those guidebook attractions, but I grew tired of the oppressive glamour and switched to the other side of the building where I gaze out over Jersey and air pollution. There are four "Deluxe Personal Domiciles" on each floor. (The building is a co-op.) Most of the people who live here are account executives, ad men or various other upwardly mobile middle-class types, willing to pay an exorbitant price for what they think is a prestige address. Like one man who owns a small chain of drugstores in Passaic. Or another across the hall who just divorced his wife, his former secretary at his lucrative insurance agency in Newark. We don't mix. My connections are all in New York, but I moved out here to hide among the middle class. The police rarely watch this building.

1

I have four very large rooms which were decorated by my stepfather's interior decorator with a few of my own variations. The living room is Louis XIII with two full-length wall mirrors and a harpsichord. There are several elegantly upholstered easy chairs and a sofa, which sometimes make me uncomfortable but are great conversation pieces at parties, especially when my guests are reluctant to sit down on them. On the wall is a medium-sized Canaletto—a detailed Venetian scene lent to me also by my stepfather, although I suspect he has forgotten it is here. I study this painting very closely. Everything is so carefully ordered. The world poses no threat to the eye as the lines of perspective move off in careful parallel to an obvious vanishing point. Men stand in sedate groups of twos and threes as a gondola crosses their path in perfect harmony with the larger scene. I am touching the surface of the painting now to see if the falling temperature—it is sixty-one—is affecting it adversely. If, by some chance, the temperature in the apartment goes below freezing at night, the paint might crack, the gondolier might fall in flakes onto the floor.

The other rooms are the study, bedroom and kitchen. The study is lined with books, most of which I confess I have not read, but my friends enjoy them when they visit, and I realized long ago that a man is judged to some extent by the choice of his library. I keep a lot of books on sexology from Krafft-Ebing and Theodor Reik to those uninformative marriage manuals you get from clipping a coupon from *The New York Times Book Review* and sending ten dollars, money back if not completely satisfied. Also I have several books on drugs and psychedelic experience in general, including *The Tibetan Book of the Dead*. Beyond this shelving, the study contains a modern sofa, a desk and a Braque—no more.

The bedroom is also simple and modern. There is a television and a chest of drawers with a matching valet set. The room is dominated by a good-sized double bed which is occupied at present by a corpse. My stepfather left no paintings for this room, so my magnetic bulletin board provides the visual diversion.

The bathroom is a bathroom; the kitchen, a kitchen.

I do not do anything for a living. I graduated from college about two and a half years ago and am still trying to sort myself out. I went to a psychoanalyst four days a week up until last

2

month when the analyst told me some things I didn't want to hear and I walked out. I suppose I'll find another one. My parents (I say parents in the plural; I've had four already) are or were professional people—city planners, engineers, modern women and so forth. Their parents, particularly one of them, were immigrants who did anything they could to make a buck. They amassed millions by means I will not enumerate here but by standard means available to racketeers of the 1930's. My parents were lucky enough to have something immoral to rebel against. They were the clean-up, whisk-away under the carpet generation. Where once stood a bootlegger, now stands a corporate executive. What does this evolutionary process leave me? The leftovers of a semi-rectified family. I could not continue on in the tradition. I am not a Kennedy or a Roosevelt. I could be an artist or a criminal, but those professions take too much courage, so I have floundered about for the past few years, leaning toward one and leaning toward the other without giving myself to either. But now, through a grotesque piece of luck, I have found my dual métier.

I have made my posh Hudson apartment into an icebox. Ideally, it should be about the temperature of a railroad cattle car (the thermostat now reads fifty-nine) since that is the kind of material I wish to preserve. Stretched out on the bed is the corpse of my girl friend Jennifer Da Silva. She was killed accidentally when I applied heroin as an antidote to the overdose of amphetamine she had taken. She was dancing about, wildly threatening suicide and, two minutes later, saying that she was having the most beautiful experience of her life. I was not unprepared for such an occurrence. I had seen it in others, even felt it myself—these tremendous manic-depressive swings taking place within a period of several minutes. But Jennifer danced dangerously close to the window. I had to quiet her down. I admit, too, that I was annoyed with her. I was not nearly as high myself and suffered from the jealousy one sometimes feels about someone else's private experiences. Perhaps that is why I injected more heroin than I might normally have given her. I do not care to speculate about this just now.

When I saw what had happened, I propped Jennifer up on the bed, turned the air conditioner at first to medium-cool, and left the apartment. I drove across the upper deck of Washington Bridge, having a coupon clipped from my book at the toll

3

booth. (Discount ticket books are available to commuters and others frequently using the bridge.) I parked my car inconspicuously on a quiet street and taxied down to Phil's Philadelphia, a kind of phony bistro on Madison in the Sixties. I ordered a drink and looked around me, pleased with the thought that I was now a murderer, albeit an inadvertent one. None of our crowd was around. It was too early in the day. I knew one of the waitresses, but made no signal to her. Somehow I felt that in my new status as killer I should remain aloof. People whose company I solicited must now come to me. I no longer loved Jennifer; I hardly even thought of her. I thought more of my new status...what it might mean to me. It was then that I got the idea for this diary. I had always been held back from writing by a feeling of futility. No one would ever read what I had written, so what was the sense of it. I realized my talent was limited, or at least that I would never work hard enough to develop it. But here was a ready-made situation. I am a killer and could write the diary of a killer—even if only by accident. I could follow closely the events from the act itself until my capture and record them in a notebook, once a day, giving an accurate picture of the changes of the frame of mind of a fugitive from justice. Not that I think I will be captured, quite the contrary; but even if I remain free, I can publish the document years later, under a pseudonym perhaps, or in a foreign country.

Most men, after all, want to bare witness to their own lives. It is just that most of them, deep down, think their own lives are not worth the trouble.

I returned to the apartment, opened the door and sniffed about. I was looking for early telltale signs of decaying flesh. There were none, but the temperature of the room seemed not to have changed significantly. It was then that I turned the air conditioner up to high and turned off the thermostat. I could live in this refrigerator if I had to. I have an electric blanket which I removed from the bed before I propped up the body. I have several good winter coats. I have a down-lined sleeping bag. In short, I have everything money can buy, because I have all the money I need. My grandfather's estate—he was the racketeer—provided me with a personal income of sixteen thousand dollars a year as well as complete control of twelve thousand shares of United Merchants & Manufacturers—22¼ the last time I looked, which was nine months ago. Any funds I might need beyond that are at my disposal. We are a large family. Old Max, that was my grandfather's name, had seven children—five boys and two girls. They were a pretty close-knit bunch when they were growing up and trying to blot out the nefarious connections in the family name, but now they have split up. All that exists of Max's multimillion dollar enterprise, Belmont Services Limited, is the money and my second cousin Selma's piddling vestige, Client Services, Inc. Most of the family has gone to Los Angeles where four of the brothers have joined together to produce advertising films for television. They represent a lot of cleansers and cigarettes and that kind of thing. My father, the fifth brother, didn't go with them. He stayed in New York to manage some oil interests that Max bought out, principally in the Middle East. When I was eight, my father walked out on my mother and went to Argentina to drill some wells. He never came back and I have seen him only twice since then. My mother remarried, this time to Maurice Hertzberg, a city planner. He thinks he's done a lot for me, bringing me into the world of the art lover and sophisticated phony. After all, I received my bachelor's degree in American Studies from one of our country's most distinguished men's colleges. I am also a graduate of one of the most highly regarded coeducational schools in New York. If there is one thing that the best in progressive education can do, it can make us (for here I must identify myself with the best and worst of the tradition) able to bullshit our way through school with formidable skill and evasiveness. Some of my friends are such good bullshitters it worked against them. Teachers marked them down for being too skillful. They didn't realized that what they thought was glibness was sometimes real brilliance. But that does not refer to me.

I have decided not to barricade the door. At least for now. There is a good double locking system on the doors in this building and I made sure long ago that the elevator men gave me plenty of warning before letting anybody up here. As final protection, the door has one of those one-way peepholes. Every few minutes I get up from my desk to see if there is anyone out in the hall.

Luckily my social schedule is not very busy for the next week. No one I know of is supposed to visit, although I do, like most young men my age, have many unannounced guests. I have two appointments outside the house scheduled for tomorrow which I shall keep. One is with my connection on the lower East Side. I intend to terminate the relationship. The need for drugs seems to have drained from me entirely. I'm on to bigger kicks, it might be said. The other appointment is my weekly luncheon with my second cousin Selma, manager of a public relations firm for third-rate rock and roll groups, at the Voisin. I go mainly for the Voisin's scrumptious desserts. Selma herself can be engaging, although she does talk too much about her industrialist husband. Beyond these meetings, I must work scrupulously for the severing of all past relationships. I must do this slowly so as not to arouse suspicion. Then, once all the personal ties are broken, I will retire from sight, perhaps to an island off the coast of Spain, where I shall have a glorious career as a novelist chronicling the adventures of a fugitive from justice, yes... a murderer.

I believe I have a week to ten days before they start snooping around this apartment for Jennifer. Her aunt phoned here Tuesday and asked for her. Jennifer lives, I should say lived, at her aunt's house on the ocean outside of East Hampton. Her parents are separated, both living in Europe someplace. I think the father hangs around St. Tropez leching after young girls one-third his age. We went out to East Hampton once about a year ago (Jennifer and I went out together pretty steadily for two years, since the day after her sixteenth birthday), and I met her aunt and we drove off to visit Walt Whitman's birthplace.

Her aunt has a drawing by Canaletto which I particularly like. The gondola moves diagonally from left to right. This time two merchants eye the gondolier carefully as he poles his graceful craft. No emotions are involved here, just perspectives and esthetic realities, the hint of movement on a guided line.

But Martha Da Silva, Jennifer's aunt, and I had little in common, although she was once an actress at the Dock Street Theatre in Charleston. She did not even like the drawing and kept it in their foyer merely because of its value. She thought, somehow, that I was the ne'er-do-well son of a distinguished family. She did not know that those people she thought distinguished were merely rebels against immorality or more particularly against a macabre and self-serving form of amorality. Jennifer would run away from the Hamptons from

6

time to time, usually once every two weeks, and stay away for short periods of time, sometimes as long as three weeks. Martha would call me under those circumstances to see how Jennifer was getting on. She didn't much care, I suppose, but if something bad or worthy of publicity happened to Jennifer, her father, either in a fit of guilt or in fear of besmirching his business image, might have a few nasty words for his sister.

When Jennifer arrived at my apartment this last time, she said she had left home forever. I believed her, too. Usually she had continued going to school while she was here. She went to the Three Caskets School surrounded by two well-known art galleries in the East Fifties. It's kind of a prep school for Upper Bohemian misfits, most of whom think they are bright but really aren't. It's sort of sad. They come to class once a year with an unassigned book by Sartre or Camus or somebody and expect everyone to acknowledge their great intellect. Actually they only read about halfway through the books and then lose them shopping for suede coats in Lord and Taylor's. Meanwhile most of them wind up having to retake sophomore English and read *Silas Marner* for the second time. This time they might finish it.

Jennifer said she wouldn't go to school anymore. After a week or so the school must have called Aunt Martha and I suppose that's why she called me earlier than usual. She was filled with tough words about how Jennifer had better go to school. She kept me on the phone for so long I almost put Jennifer on, but just then Martha swore resignedly and I heard a click on the other end. Jennifer looked very forlorn on the sofa and for the first time, when I looked at her, I didn't feel lucky to have such a hip, good-looking girl friend. There was something sad and immature about her, not anything like when I first met her. That was when I was traveling through Europe a couple of summers ago with my mother, just about six months before she married Hertzberg. We had visited Spain and then flown to Rome for a month in Italy. We made our way up to Florence and then over the coast to Viareggio, and then up via Genoa to Milan and then to Venice.

The apartment is beginning to cool off now. I have taken my pen and pad into the bedroom where I am slipping on a fall coat and ski parka. Actually this is my favorite coat and, although I have a large wardrobe, I like to wear it as much as I can.

Sometimes I will keep it out from September until May. It is a holdover from my college days. I went to a college where everybody was a skier and I didn't want to be recognized as a rich kid. That partially explains why I drove a two-year-old Fairlane convertible when I could have driven the best in foreign sportscars, a Porsche or a Bugatti or some limited-model Italian car that no one had heard of. I could fly over to the factory for a weekend and test-drive it on the spot, if I wanted to. The jacket is frayed at the edges, but I don't think I will ever get a replacement. Someday it will get so bad that I cannot wear it, but I shall never throw it away. It will have a place in my closet next to a cashmere suit from Chipp and Sons or some special mod fashions I might by on Carnaby Street in London.

I must make out a short list of the people who might cross the Hudson and visit me here. I shall begin first with those who have visited here recently. There is Henderson, an actor, and Lorraine, his girl friend. Yvonne, Jennifer's obese friend from the Three Caskets School, who sometimes comes up here looking for her. Shahib Lewis. Bruce, a graduate student in graphics at Yale, who thinks he's quite the ladies' man. Larry Dolci, the connection, but I'm going to see him tomorrow first. My mother, once in a blue moon. And Ornstein, an old college acquaintance I never liked too much. He's now a writer and I think he's using me as a subject in a play, but if he found out what I was doing he wouldn't say anything. He owes me too much. Of course there are all those people from last year when I had some huge parties over at my second cousin's apartment while she was away and gave out all that free marijuana, but so far I've hardly had any direct contact with any of them. They are a peculiar breed of fair-weather friend. I shall make little name cards for each of these people who are likely to appear here and place them on my magnetic board. I shall not confuse them with the names already there (Ngo Dinh Diem, Ho Chi Minh, Nguyen Cao Ky, Tri Thrich Quang, Nguyen Quoc Dinh, Bao Dai, Pham Ngoh Thach and Cuong De—all prominent figures in the Southeast Asian crisis). They are the teams in a game of solitaire ping-pong I play with myself on a board which returns the ball automatically. They were on sale at Abercrombie and Fitch a few years ago as a Christmas gift for the man who has everything. Hit with a normal trajectory, the ball bounces down and is returned to you in the usual fashion. I alternate sides and

8

play no favorites. That Ho Chi Minh and Nguyen Cao Ky are two and three in the rankings and are, at this writing, the ranking leaders of North and South Viet Nam, I can only ascribe to the laws of chance or the intervention of some divine providence.

But when I see the others whose names I have written, I shall tell them, at the precise moment we are to part company, that I have moved from my apartment, and then be gone, omitting, as if by accident, the address of my new residence. They will assume they can ask me another time, perhaps when they next see me at the Philadelphia. Only I will be wary. I will watch carefully for them making sure we do not cross paths and then I will have disappeared from sight. Jennifer, it will be thought, has left the country with me, whereas instead she will study the growth of algae at the bottom of the East River. No, no. I don't think I'll leave her there. I'll have to find some place less predictable. I have heard that there are alligators living in the New York sewers. New Yorkers on vacation in Miami buy a baby for a dollar or two at one of the alligator farms. When they return, their pet, usually named for a character in "Pogo," grows a little too large for family adoration and is dumped in a moment of frustration (they had intended to donate it to the zoo) down the guest toilet. A few years ago a maintenance man was eaten alive by an alligator in the New York sewers. Since then city employees have been more cautious. But what an excellent method of body disposal for the master criminal. If I could only find a way.

That summer two years ago when we met, I was probably the most unhappy I had ever been. My mother and I had been traveling for nearly two months. We stayed in the finest hotel in each city or resort. There were very few people my age— either younger children staying with their families or young genius executives with their wives, all several years my senior and with interests far distant from mine. My mother found many friends and dancing partners, old and new. She is not a beautiful woman, but she knows how to carry herself and she has the kind of aggressiveness that can attract men quickly in foreign places. I would drink a lot in the lounges in the evenings as she would dance with one gentleman or another and then finally with me, commenting on who the man was and whether she thought he was being honest about himself. I scarcely cared.

9

In Viareggio a girl around twenty was staying at the same hotel with her mother. I saw her and told my mother I thought she was attractive, but she left that night and I hadn't had the courage or the energy to approach her during the tea dancing, although I was sure she was eying me the whole time. I never got to strike out on my own in those towns because I felt that it was my responsibility to take care of my mother at night and see that she was entertained. I admit that I was not great entertainment. I tended to be moody and say nasty things about the help, but at least I provided her with the good grace of an escort before she could find one of her own, a vice president from the Cunard Lines or a vacationing Italian automobile exporter.

I am very tired. The activities of the day have been fatiguing. We always strain our muscles when we do something we have never done before. And besides, I have never written this much in one day. Perhaps I shall have more to say tomorrow. I strive only to be honest in my story and tell what happened and my reactions as accurately as I can. To prove that I do not embellish the facts on my own behalf, I shall admit to you that I am not handsome. I am also rather short, slightly under five-foot six and insecure, so my psychiatrist used to say or rather, as he would have it, helped me realize. My bushy black eyebrows, black eyes and high forehead give me a slightly simian appearance—and a close look at the upper part of my mouth will show the hint of a harelip. A birthmark is visible at the point of my chin. But to know these things about yourself does not help. They are still there and the mass of humanity is still beyond as a basis for comparison.

I always play a game of solitaire ping-pong at the end of the day. Tonight it is Pham Ngoh Thach against Nguyen Quoc Dinh. Thach wished to challenge Tri Thrich Quang, but you are only allowed to challenge two ahead on the ladder.

My players are not always from Viet Nam. Last year I named them after famous rabbis in the *Talmud* and the *Midrash*. And the year before that after characters in certain Shakespearean plays. Perhaps next they will be Arab chieftains. I heard over the car radio today of the new massing of troops in the Middle East.

The apartment is now very cold. I have a comforter wrapped around me. I lean over to my left and turn the electric blanket up to hot. And slide beneath it.

Second Day...

This morning was one of the most beautiful experiences of my life. I woke up completely refreshed, not remembering a thing I had dreamed. Not the slightest touch of a cobweb lodged in my mind. I was clean. The windows were all frosted over and the morning light made a rainbow pattern as it shined through. I was very snug in my electric blanket, an efficient GE double bed model. I felt a little like I was roughing it or camping with the room temperature now forty-four, while I soothed myself in my long underwear under the hot blanket. I didn't want to get out. (The corpse, by the way, was propped up in the bathtub. A cliché, I admit, but I got sleepy very fast last night. I must have been enervated by my experience.) The glass of water on the headboard had not frozen and I could see the temperature did not go below freezing. I guess I experienced one of those few minutes of harmony that come along every two or three years. All my life had fallen into place. I understood who I was and what I had to do. With my right hand I reached for my slippers, put them on and then dashed for my robe. It was cold. But I didn't care. I was active in body and mind. Within minutes I had washed, shaved, dressed and left the house. Not until I was downstairs did I realized it was seven in the morning.

I accomplished a lot during the day after those first few hours I had to kill before everybody woke up. First I went to downtown New York to see Larry Dolci at his apartment on Second Street and Avenue B. I was glad it was so early, because it was hard to get a hold of Larry sometimes. And I knew just what I could tell him that would keep him as far away from my apartment as I could want. I knocked on his door. In a few seconds Larry appeared. He kept the chain latch on. He was so sleepy I didn't think he could recognize me, but he nodded. He must have thought I needed some heroin in a hurry and was contemplating how much money he could take me for, his uptown, rich kid patsy. It was strange to see Larry Dolci in pajama bottoms. He must have thought so, too, because he told

11

me to wait outside. Five minutes later he called to met to enter. The door was unlatched and there was Dolci standing in the corner of the room wearing a spun silk smoking jacket with a cigarette in a gold holder dangling from his mouth. He led me through the austere entry room, obviously a front, into his posh sitting room. The walls were sprayed with gold flecks and the chaise lounge upholstered in ermine. Larry Dolci went in big for ostentation.

"Up and at it early this morning, aren't we?" he said.

"Yes, I couldn't sleep."

"I see...Mansueto."

A huge Mafia-type goon entered and Dolci told him to bring us some coffee. Each time I see him he has a different bodyguard. Shahib Lewis tells me he is rising very fast in the ranks.

"I hope you like Italian coffee. It's very strong."

"Two lumps," I said, conscious of the fact that I was handling myself very well.

"What brings you here, Marcus? It's too early in the morning to prolong the preliminaries."

"I thought I should inform you of something."

"I'm glad you have my best interest at heart," he said.

"I thought you'd appreciate my keeping you posted."

"If you have something to say, say it."

"I wanted to tell you so that you would know all."

I was beginning to address him like a parent or teacher or someone like that, although he was one or two years younger than I.

"Thank you for your consideration."

"I just thought I'd warn you that the narcotic's bulls are watching my house. They must be checking on who's going in and out. I think I'll stay clean for awhile and you'd better stay clear of the apartment."

"Perhaps they followed you here?" he suggested.

Mansueto brought the coffee. Dolci put two lumps in mine; he took his black.

"No, no. I got up real early, crossed the bridge and drove to the vicinity of Fordham University, took a taxi up to Jerome Avenue and then took a subway down from there, changing twice. There was no one at all on the platform the second time I changed."

"An interesting story . . . make a note of Mr. Rottner's story, Mansueto."

Mansueto made a note of it. Dolci stood up. I could smell the scent of expensive cologne. I wondered how he had been able to prepare himself so impeccably in the short time I stood outside the door. He led me out.

"As a good customer, may I ask you a personal question?"

Dolci stopped for a second, as if weighing whether he should allow this intrusion. He nodded.

"How old are you?"

"Nineteen. This was a birthday present from my mother," he said, showing me the jacket.

On the street, I smiled, experiencing once again the exhilaration of a successful criminal. I had never acted so efficiently, though so quickly. Dolci was deceived. Step by step, I continued my journey. I took a cab uptown again and stopped in at the Philadelphia to see if any of the crowd was there. I could warn them off. The only one I saw was Ornstein who was finishing his brunch of scrambled eggs, lox and bagels with a glass of beer. He always ate the same thing at the same hour of every day. Even his recreation was programed. When I arrived he was about to leave. He drank the end of his beer, nodded to me, signed his check and exited. For all that he owes me, he didn't say a word. I left two minutes later for lunch with Cousin Selma at the Voisin. We arrived at the marquee simultaneously.

"The same table as usual, Mrs. Schlicht and Mr. Rottner?" said the maitre d'. That was my second cousin's married name. My name has undergone many changes, but I formalized Rottner when I reached twenty-one in honor of my grandfather.

My cousin is very thin and always wears a large red hat which flops around her face like a pair of kangaroo ears. She eats everything in sight and talks incessantly, mostly she loves to gossip because she thinks she's really in the thick of show business. She runs Client Services Incorporated which does public relations for rock and roll singers and tap dancers.

Client Services Incorporated is the reincarnation of Grandpa Max's old business, Belmont Enterprises, only Belmont Enterprises never bothered with young acne-faced entertainers who spend their lives singing in Italian supper clubs in the East Bronx. Grandpa Max had some of the biggest liquor, meat and oil concerns as his clients. But they all suspended their accounts just before the Second World War when Max was arrested for perjury in a federal investigation of the liquor industry. He had amassed one of the largest fortunes in America by whitewashing the criminal reputations of bootleggers after Prohibition so they could take their rightful places as the captains of the liquor industry. Max made America think bathtub gin was a cross between mother's milk and mineral water. Cousin Selma was the only one of her generation who didn't run from the public relations business after the liquidation of Belmont Enterprises. She salvaged an office near Tin Pan Alley and started to assemble the aforementioned sallow faces. The business failed miserably, but that didn't matter. She still had her share of Rottner millions and her husband could support the entire Polish Army on his own anyway. Old Max had a special place in his heart for Selma because when she was sixteen or so she told her uncle she wanted to set up a literary salon. Now she has to content herself with some Bar Mitzvah bass player-or-other instead of Baudelaire, but such are the times.

I didn't have to read the menu at the Voisin. I knew everything on it and Alain, our waiter, would have told us if they had had any specials.

"Heffie," that's my cousin's affectionate name for her husband Harold Schlicht, "Heffie's business is booming. You know the hat department? Well, he was the first manufacturer in this country to produce multicolored berets. It seemed like a wasted by-product. Deadwood. He'd get an order for ten reds when someone wanted to have a Basque-style party or something like that. But now with the war and Sergeant Barry Sadler's hit song, green berets have become his best selling product since Daniel Boone coonskin caps, and the way the war is going it may be longer lasting. I'll tell you confidentially..."

She looked cautiously around the room to make sure no one was listening.

"He may clear a million-dollar profit in green berets alone this year. That's more war profiteering than any of your muckrakers of the Thirties could have dreamed of. Lincoln Steffens would turn over in his grave."

She thought she was showing her erudition by bringing in Lincoln Steffens. What a joke.

"How's Jennifer?"

14

Selma delighted in asking me about Jennifer. Because of the nature of her work, she feels she is more qualified than others to communicate with the younger generation. One need only ask them about their problems.

"Oh, she's been keeping kind of quiet," I replied rather cryptically. Selma smiled, thinking she was communicating deeply through her quick and easy knowledge of contemporary slang. Imagine. Here I was already five years beyond being a teen-ager.

"She's a nice girl, but don't you think she's a little too young for you? Not that relative age is so important, but she might slow your growth as an individual. Sometimes you're hiding from yourself when you become involved with someone much younger than you."

It's funny. I've always thought of Jennifer and me as the same age, although I've always known her chronological age. The first day I met her was her sixteenth birthday. She was in Venice with her family staying at the same hotel we were, the Royal Danieli. I was eating dinner with my mother at the rooftop restaurant at the mouth of the Grand Canal. The sunset bounced a crimson light off the water and the high windows of the mansions along the canal. An elegant waiter in a tuxedo with ruffled shirtfront was serving us fettucini from under golden covers. The hotel band and the bands going by in small motor barges below rivaled each other in the saccharine playing of old Italian melodies on accordion and violin. My second glass of wine was in the process of mixing with its mate and two martinis. My mother and I had nothing to say to each other. Venice was beautiful, but it was a hollow shell. The musicians conspired to heighten the disharmony. Two old accordionists stood below playing "Santa Lucia," while the band behind us tried a medium tempo "Deep Purple."

"My standing offer still goes, Marcus. You don't have to be so proud. Come to work for us at Client Services and the job's yours. Better still, I've found something more interesting for you. You took an Eastern religions course in college, didn't you? Well, a group called The Flaming Spears, you may have heard of them, is looking for someone to write lyrics for Raga Rock songs they compose on the sitar. What makes them unique is they want the lyrics to relate to the original spirit of the Oriental faiths. Ergo, you would do something on Buddhism or

15

Hinduism or Shinto with a little bit of the modern love interest," said Selma, carefully slicing some paté.

"I told you my analyst said I shouldn't make any commitments as yet. I'm not ready for it. I have to get my past life sorted out before I can move into the future...I think I'll have the vichyssoise and the capon."

Santa Lucia, Santa Lucia...

I looked into the right corner of that penthouse garden restuarant two and a half years ago and saw a girl eating dinner with her parents. Her parents sat sideways and she had her back to me. All I could see was her beautiful hair. That was always her best feature, chestnut hair which came all the way down to her waist that she would wrap around her face sometimes and play peek-a-boo. The waiter was bringing them a bottle of champagne. It was some kind of celebration, but I could see they weren't too happy with each other. The mother's head was tilted away from the others, although she had no interest in the view. The father was making sure the waiter only poured the girl a half glass of champagne. The girl was tapping on the plate with her silverware. A conventional family scene. The father raised his glass in toast to the daughter. The mother reluctantly turned toward them and raised hers halfway. "Happy birthday, Jennifer, sweet sixteen," said the father. The mother resumed her canal vigil.

The waiter brought us the first course: my vichyssoise and Selma's langouste something or other. I always lived for the desserts at the Voisin anyway.

"I'll pay for the lunch today," I said.

"What's the occasion?"

"I've just come into an inheritance."

"Funny man," Selma said, placing an empty langouste shell in her butter dish. A waiter hovered behind us, ready to pounce with his water pitcher should he see a slight decrease in the level of the glasses.

My mother was carefully studying the penthouse for likely prey. It was already our second night in Venice and she had found no one to set her sights on. I remarked how the girl across the way was having a dull "Sweet Sixteen," but she didn't seem to notice.

16

Why does Selma always keep that infernal hat on while she's eating? It's almost like she's wearing a public relations merit badge.

That beautiful chestnut hair fell over the back of the chair. I took it upon myself to give her a sweet sixteen. I called the waiter over and asked him to select the most elegant cake he could find, put sixteen candles on it, and send it to her table with my compliments. He wheeled over a massive rum cake, flambeau, a beautiful blue flame with sixteen green sparklers. The spongy cake just oozed rum. My heart pounded. I had never done anything like that before.

The Voisin is known the world over for its desserts, mostly pastries. Today there were tarts, and cream puffs, éclairs of all varieties, napoleons, mocha and strawberry chiffon cakes and all order of goo for which you can never remember the name but just point your finger.

"Didn't your mother tell me you stopped seeing your psychiatrist?"

"Yes, I did. I don't think he understood."

That approach always evokes sympathy from Selma.

"I see your point. But it negates his opinion about my job offer. He can't tell you when you're ready to commit yourself to anything when he's not your doctor anymore."

Selma was working on a fish specialty with mornay sauce.

Jennifer's expression when that cake arrived was so vivid, it is hard to imagine that she is departed from us. She was aghast. Her face contorted. She told me later that she was surprised, pleased and at once suspicious that it was some trick of her father's to get her to come back and live with him. But she's dead now. Who killed Jennifer? Jennifer couldn't tell us. She always put the blame on the first one in sight. I realized it that first night when we were riding together in a gondola and she asked the gondolier to take us to Milan. At first I thought she was kidding and the gondolier couldn't speak English anyway.

"Take us to Milan," she said, swinging her pocketbook in the air.

Our young Venetian guide looked very confused. I laughed and put my arms around her. She must have thought I liked the idea.

"Milano. Milano," she said, propelling the boat with an imaginary paddle.

The gondolier began to laugh, too, and say *"Milano. Milano. Impossibile, impossibile."*

Jennifer became very annoyed and kept insisting he paddle us to the other city. He continued to laugh. She started to sulk and then began to curse the gondolier in English words he could understand, so we had to disembark. There was no malice in this. She was just spoiled. People make a mistake. Spoiled children aren't malicious. Sometimes, they're very sweet.

When the cake arrived, the waiter pointed in my direction. I suppose I blushed. The father smiled benignly; Jennifer eyed me curiously. The mother turned around for a second and then turned back and resumed her vigil. The father got up and came over to our table. He asked if we would join in the celebration of his daughter's sixteenth birthday. The waiter joined the tables together. Jennifer hadn't said a word. I liked that about her. The father asked what college I went to—he was that type—and was pretty impressed. I had to laugh. The cake was good. The mother wasn't looking at us. She stared out across the canal.

"Are you going to find a new psychiatrist?" asked Selma.

"Eventually. I think I'll let myself drift for a while first. Build self-reliance. I was toying with the idea of trying yoga for inner strength."

"Oriental cultism is going to be the new phase. You should see what they do with it in California. You wouldn't believe it."

"Selma, do you enjoy doing public relations for those idiots?"

"What do you mean?"

"You should live in New Jersey, the way I do, away from it all."

"And waste my life?"

"You must really be hard up to live a glamorous life."

"Marcus, keep your voice down."

Selma was nervously fingering the edge of her plate with one hand and her floppy hat with the other. She continued:

"Look, Marcus, I'm going to get you a psychiatrist myself."

"That's a nice thing to say."

"I only have your best interests at heart."

"Like your Uncle Max used to say, Selma—the importance of the outside view.

18

She didn't like my sarcasm. That was Max Rottner's favorite slogan. He adopted it after it helped him win the Plattsburgh Oil account in 1931. Public relations wasn't such a universally accepted idea in those days, so when Max had suggested the services of Belmont to this yahoo from Plattsburgh, he was told any decent business could take care of its own publicity. Only the yahoo, Mr. Locumtide is the name usually given him by the family, was about to address an international convention of oil tycoons. He took five steps toward the lectern when Max called to him. "Excuse me, Mr. Locumtide, but I believe your fly is opened." "Thank you, Mr. Rottner," was the sheepish reply. "That sir," said my grandfather, "is the importance of the outside view." A slogan and a million-dollar account were born.

The last piece of fish was on the way to Selma's mouth, smothered in mornay sauce. She said: "I'm going to send the first psychiatrist I can find up to your apartment."

"I wouldn't be sending anyone up to my apartment just now. It's very cold. Something's gone wrong with the thermostat control and the air conditioner stays on all day and the heater doesn't work. I slept last night in a sweater with the electric blanket up to high. I've been out since seven o'clock this morning."

"I'm sure they've already fixed it."

"Every apartment in the house is fouled. It may take days."

I wasn't sure she was believing this, but the waiter arrived in time to interrupt any further questions. He took our plates and brought the dessert tray.

Jennifer didn't eat any of the cake. Her father was the big eater of the family. When he was on his third, he suggested I take Jennifer out for a night on the town. She was sixteen now and entitled to it. Somehow I had the impression he was looking at my mother's legs. Jennifer wore those crisscrossed stockings that all New York girls were wearing at that time. The mother looked out across the canal. Jennifer still hadn't said a word. Dutifully, she stood up and followed me. My mother opened her pocketbook and put a fifty-dollar traveler's check in my hand, a silly gesture with maternal overtones, considering she knew full well that I had plenty of my own and had exactly four hundred and twenty in my pocket at the moment. I looked at Jennifer for her reaction. She remained impassive.

Leaving a building along the Grand Canal has such a strange quality. The stranger forgets that he is surrounded by water unless he is looking directly at it. When he reaches the front door of his hotel he expects to be greeted by the rush of Unter den Linden or the Champs Elysées or the Gran Via, but instead there is only that murky canal poisoned by centuries of Venetian refuse, and two barber poles in slightly tarnished red and white, where the seedily romantic gondolier moors his boat. On summer nights, large gondolas with small orchestras go by, decked in flowers and colored lights. Some of these carry passengers. I do not know how the others support themselves. When the doorman called us a gondola, I turned fully to Jennifer for the first time in my life. She was crying. All the frustration of being cooped up by parents on the verge of divorce welled up from within her. And it came from within me, too. I cried and she started to laugh. It was a laugh of pure understanding, the kind of laugh that never hurts the other party but puts them in sympathy with the one making fun of them.

We rode for a long time without speaking. We were playing the game of those unspoken Hollywood friendships which blossom into something much more significant than those made through mundane verbal approaches. Jennifer was the first to break the silence.

"I'll never go to Europe again with anyone but you," she said. "You've made me so happy taking me away from there."

It was a Hollywood night.

I chose a large cream puff from the dessert tray. Selma chose a napoleon, or mille-feuille, as they call it at the Voisin. She always has one. I shift around—sometimes this rare delight, sometimes that. Cream puffs were Jennifer's favorite, and perhaps that is why I picked one this time. Selma waits the whole meal for her napoleon. The sight of it may have made her forget her promise to arrange an appointment for me with a new psychiatrist. Selma knows lots of fancy, highbrow psychiatrists. This one was Marilyn Monroe's analyst and that one psychoanalyzed Jackson Pollock. I even suspect that Selma blew pot once just to be in with the literary set, but she'd never tell her husband about it.

Selma had two glasses of Cointreau after lunch and left me in a haze. I drove home to the apartment and started telephoning old acquaintances, telling some that I was leaving town for

20

a while and others that my phone was being disconnected because I was in the process of moving. I stood huddled over the telephone, blowing icy smoke into the air, leafing through my address book and one by one checking off the numbers. Two old friends were married, four numbers were disconnected, one hung up on me and couldn't remember who I was. I suppose if I had mentioned paintings and money and free marijuana the memory would have come back, but that's a little obvious. I stopped at Ornstein's name, wondering whether to call him with the others. With Ornstein everything had to be perfect, the slightest inflection in my voice could give the game away. He was such a natural snoop. I wonder what kind of a character he's going to make me in his novel, or is it a play? I have a feeling he hates me. I decided not to call. It would be better to catch him in a free moment at the Philadelphia or on the street. Then, lost in his thoughts, he would just nod as I tell him I'm going to move or disappear into the Orient. Somewhere in the back of his mind he would make a note on the behavior of the underdeprived for his next novel.

There's only one person who reminds me of Ornstein and that's my grandfather. They both knew what they wanted— or in the case of Ornstein, still knows. The only thing that's hazy to me in the background of Grandfather Max is why he came to this country. It might have been a pogrom—they often talked of religious discrimination—but that was why he went from Poland to Germany in the first place, and not even he could predict the rise of the Nazis ten years before World War I. I picture him like the hero of the movie *America, America*, a kind of tough young punk with a lot more guts and brains than the rest of the family. A youth willing to sacrifice everything to have his chance in America. He was riding an arrow to the sky.

I hardly remember what he looked like. I was five years old when he died in jail for perjury. The cause of death was never made clear. I wasn't supposed to know about that when I was young. Nobody even talks to me about it now and they change the subject when I bring it up myself. Sometimes I suspect he died of a nervous condition like epilepsy.

Max arrived in this country with his devoted wife, Rose. She was a tiny woman from the neighboring village in

Poland. Max was scarcely over five feet himself, a little Napoleon. He carried a cane bought in Paris as his boat pulled into New York harbor. Max always tried to look rich, even in those early days when he didn't have a penny. That is why I, being born rich, try to look poor. Rose carried their only valuable possession, an exquisite centerpiece of Dresden china. The top was ornamented with a trio of musicians playing a medley of country tunes. Rose clutched a box with the centerpiece to her breast as she leaned over the rail. The boat was easing into the pier on Ellis Island. She could see thousands of yelling, screaming immigrants pushing at the gates. Max stood complacently by her. His dream was being realized. Old women from Galicia, young tradesmen from Latvia, Swedes, Poles, even Latins pushed at their backs. The boat lurched forward and the centerpiece hurtled a hundred feet into the mouth of the East River. The last vestige of the Old Country sank before arrival. Very neat and poetic, almost incredible, but I choose to believe it. My father's brothers and sisters used to laugh about that. Maybe it's a ritual of self-justification. There certainly isn't any of the Old World left in them, despite the fact that at least three of the seven are in Europe every summer. They keep the others well supplied with Lacoste shirts for Los Angeles golf wear.

As I thought of Max, Ornstein called. I wonder why I always think of them together. Where Max was a spendthrift, Ornstein is austere. Max was expansive, Ornstein is calculating, withdrawn.

"Hello, this is Ornstein."

"Hello."

"Is anything wrong with you?"

"Don't be silly."

"You needn't yell."

"I wasn't yelling."

"I beg your pardon. I thought I detected a higher pitch in your voice. Are you sure nothing is wrong?"

"What could be wrong?"

"At the Philadelphia today you were not your usual self."

"Well, I've had a cold all day, Sigmund."

"Wouldn't you like me to come over and see to things?"

22

Here I knew that he just wanted to observe me, to see how I would behave under various stimuli.

"Marcus, are you still there?"

"Yes, yes, I'm still here. Under no circumstances is anyone to come to my apartment."

"Why not?"

"The air conditioner isn't working."

"Why should it? It's still early spring."

"Well, it wouldn't work if I needed it."

"I'm coming out to Jersey, Marcus."

"I will instruct the elevator man not to let you up."

"I'll come by the stairs."

"The door will remain locked."

"Marcus, this is your old friend Sigmund Ornstein from the college on the hill. I'm not out to hurt you . . . Why don't we meet tomorrow at the old running track in Van Cortland Park? We'll remember the old days at dancing school and all that jazz about rich Jewish kids growing up in Manhattan . . . Come on, I'll make it my personal interest to cheer you up."

"All right, nine A.M."

"I can't go any place at that hour. I'm writing from six to ten. Since when do you, the heir of the Rottners, awake before noon?"

"I'll be there whenever you arrive."

Amenities exchanged. Click. Click.

What could I do? I couldn't refuse. That would arouse too much suspicion.

I am about to turn out the light. Ho Chi Minh and Nguyen Cao Ky have just finished an animated game of ping-pong as befits their rival stations as leaders of the North and South. Ky won, but in order to mirror closely the real-life action, I have given him assistance from American "advisers" in the form of a top-spin backhand.

Third Day...

Something very bad happened to me today, but just to prove that I am completely in control, I will first resume my exploration of the past, my personal delving into the dark corners of my soul, my purgation. The tensions of the moment will not deter me.

What concerned Jennifer and me most when we toured the by-ways and *riis* of Venice was whether we had begun something long and special or just a short interlude in a romantic setting. We knew that we could see each other easily when we returned. We lived in the same area, even had a few mutual friends. All this was foremost in our thoughts, but we never mentioned it. We moved dutifully about Venice from the Bridge of Sighs to Saint Mark's Cathedral to the island where they blow the glass. There I bought Jennifer a hand-blown elephant of pink glass. She was very harsh with the poor Venetian artisan, who didn't know that much English, trying to make sure that it was well packed and sent to the correct address. I wasn't sure why she cared so much. I had bought it for her out of a sense of traveler's duty. In Venice you buy Venetian blown glass. I began to notice something in her behavior; I can't say what it was. When she looked at me, she wanted me to stay there. Perhaps that cheap piece of glass meant something to her sentimentally, or perhaps she was just showing that impatient frustration with foreigners which comes from tour-ing the continent against your will because one parent or both needs to escape from home. Only once before had a girl looked at me that way. Her name was Ann and I was seventeen years old and spending a summer on Cape Cod with my father's mother. I don't want to write about that at all, but she really liked me and I suppose I was embarrassed. It was the same way then with Jen-nifer, only this time I wasn't embarrassed. I must have spent something like two hundred dollars that week on gondolas alone. My mother was very lonely. Jennifer and I talked all the time. All the weeks of conversation held in with parents and step-parents and near gigolos came flowing out.

She told me how her great-grandparents emigrated from Portugal and bought a rice plantation south of Charleston, South Carolina, near Beaufort and what is now Parris Island. Many Portuguese had settled there and they spoke a dialect called "geechee" (I think that's how it was spelled) which is a kind of combination Southern drawl and Portuguese. After Reconstruction, most of the family moved North and got involved with textile and shoe manufacturing in New England mill towns like Lawrence, Lowell and Manchester. Jennifer's father was a sweater manufacturer before he sold his business and moved to France. She showed me a picture of herself at the age of three wearing a light blue sweater which was used as advertising in *The New Yorker* and *Vogue*. She couldn't have been a model now. Her features were somehow too angular. When she was little, her parents were divorced.

Jennifer was an only child and they sent her back to live with her Aunt Martha between the ages of six and ten. It was then that Martha acted with the Dock Street Theatre.

I'm sorry, but I must interrupt the narrative here. I am very nervous and unable to type or print. Ornstein knows. I'm sure he knows I am hiding a dead body up here. It is eight P.M. The general apartment temperature is forty-nine, except for a small electric heater, camp-type, which I have purchased and have stationed next to my typewriter. I must do something about the body. It is too obvious propped up there in the tub. Besides, I haven't been able to take a bath or shower since the murder or death, call it what you will, not that I would want to in this freezer. Excuse me while I remove the body from the lavatory....

I have moved the body from the lavatory to the least likely place in the apartment, the inside of the harpsichord. I removed the inner-workings, broke them apart and left them out the back door for the janitor to pick up with the trash. Perhaps this seems profligate of me—after all, the harpsichord is an antique, of a very rare vintage, I am told, with some exquisite marquetry—but when it is a case of life and a death, nothing can be spared. Jennifer is small, but few would assume she could fit inside a harpsichord, especially with all the frets and plucks, or whatever they call them, within. As a final touch, I have closed the keyboard. There is a keyhole in the wood that covers the board, but I can't remember ever having found the key. I have nailed everything shut. Moving the body was not that uncomfortable. She is wrapped up in a white sheet so I never see her directly, and whatever smell of decay there may be has apparently been masked by the heavy doses of Chanel's English Leather talcum powder I douse the sheets with every morning.

I learned how much Jennifer liked perfumes and powders when we got back to New York. The first time I went to her house in East Hampton to pick her up, she wouldn't let me in because I didn't wear any cologne or after-shave lotion. I was fuming, but I drove into the village and found an open drugstore and bought a bottle of Old Spice, spilling it over me as if it were a disinfectant. When I got back to the house, Jennifer took one look at me and said,

"Old Spice. Couldn't you think of anything more original? Okay, it will have to do. Now let's go to your apartment."

I was surprised, even taken aback by her abruptness now that we were back in the States. She walked into the apartment ahead of me—another one, not the one we are in now—jumped onto the bed and said, "Now." She smelled of jasmine things and strange Oriental scents. She was a virgin, but that didn't seem to bother her. She never even mentioned it. I felt like the inexperienced partner. She smiled when it was through and then went into my superstocked bathroom and covered herself with a mixture of all the scents available.

"You smell like a sample counter at Bonwit Teller's," I said.

"My lips and mouth are Joy, my right ear Chanel Number Five, my left ear Chanel Number Eleven, my arms Tigress, my breasts Sortilège, my legs Arpege and just below the belt My Sin by Lanvin."

We giggled with a gay sense of the Oriental and lascivious.

"Which part do you like best?" she asked.

"Hmm...I prefer Arpege and My Sin."

"You have to be really nice to ever get a smell of My Sin again."

"I'll buy you a bottle myself."

"It's five dollars an ounce."

"I'll have the milkman bring it by the quart."

And we giggled some more.

Those were good times. Jennifer jumping on the bed and giggling and my talking about My Sin. They must be forgotten. The times have changed.

Will Ornstein report me to the police? I have never trusted him. I have never called him a friend, never wanted to. I never went after his company. In fact all during college he hardly ever said a word to me. I'm sure he hated my guts. He thought of me, still does I'm sure, as one of those poor little rich boys with literary aspirations. Even when we were in the sixth grade at Vernal's dancing school on East Sixty-fourth Street, I felt he looked down on me. It's true I was very shy, but he was no Beau Brummel himself. Today he just stands in the corner at parties with that conceited, all-knowing look of his, as if we were part of a comedy being enacted for his satisfaction. When we were boys of eight or nine, we were members of a group called Stan Motion's Boy's Athletic Club. They would take us on Saturdays to play basketball or football or visit Palisade's Amusement Park. Stan was Irish, but a lot of the kids in the group were Jewish, drawing, as he did, on Madison Avenue and the Eighties for most of his clientele. The Jewish kids and the Irish didn't mix that well, especially at Motion's summer camp where the differences were accentuated every Sunday morning when the Catholics went to Mass and the Jews had a couple of extra hours sleep. One summer Ornstein and I were the only Jews in our bunk so they wouldn't leave a counselor with us for those two hours. Ornstein didn't like much then though. He spent all the time reading.

It was strange when we wound up at the same college. He did a double-take on the street the first day as we passed each other. He must have been wondering how I could have been admitted into such an institution and then assumed that I was another person. It wasn't until they had a drugs scandal on campus our senior year that he came to take an interest in me.

We met this afternoon at one of Stan Motion's old stamping grounds, Van Cortland Park in the Bronx. We used to play football there. Ornstein thought he was a pretty good player. He takes everything he does seriously. He is a very intense person. He betrays this in his personal appearance, very thin and nervous with cold gray eyes and several flecks of gray in his wiry black hair, although he is only in his early twenties. Now when he writes he keeps a strict regimen and a strict diet. He also reads a certain number of books and will only allow himself a certain amount of recreation.

"How are you?" he asked.

"Fine."

"What do you mean fine? You sounded like I interrupted you in the middle of a suicide attempt on the phone last night...Are you marching in the demonstration tomorrow?"

"What demonstration?" I asked. Suicide attempts were kind of fashionable in our set and I wasn't surprised he thought I was trying one. There was a girl named Joan who lived off Fifth Avenue on Ninety-third Street. She was Ornstein's girl friend when we were in grammar school. Later she grew very fat, but still had mysterious eyes and looked something like Circe. She had an Irish Catholic boy friend who became so nervous because of her intellectual Jewish ways that he jumped out of the window from the eleventh story while she was lying in bed in the same room waiting for him. Three months later she married a bartender on the West Side—not a bartender who wanted to be a writer or a painter or something like that, just a bartender. This affected Ornstein a great deal when he was in college because he had turned into a very moral person.

"The march against the war in Viet Nam," he said. "We need all the bodies we can get out there. Wear your best suit—I guess in your case any suit will do—and meet at the Central Park Mall tomorrow at ten. I'll look for you. I think you should carry a sign 'Down with Yankee Imperialism.' It would turn your grandfather over in his grave."

"He wouldn't care. He's been called a lot worse things than an imperialist."

"Will you be there?"

"Sure. Sure."

"Now maybe I can help you," said Ornstein, leading me up toward the running path. A tough-looking blond boy with a Manhattan College jersey was running down the hill. "How's Jennifer?"

"I don't know. I haven't seen her for a while."

"What's the matter? Did you have an argument?"

"You're not getting any material out of me, Ornstein. For all I know you've got a tape recorder in your pocket." He had had a short story published in *Hudson Review* the year after he finished college. I never read it, but some friends told me that it was set in Spain, so I suppose I wasn't one of his characters.

"I heard she left home," he said.

He turned the other way and I couldn't tell whether he was being sympathetic or trying to attack me.

"I hope you two haven't had a fight. I know how much you care about her. Love is what saves us all, man."

I looked at him suspiciously.

"I guess you're surprised to see Ornstein so maudlin, but I mean it. Don't do anything to hurt Jennifer. You've gotten each other into too much trouble. You need each other."

Ornstein's warmth came from deep within him, but it was something mechanical tied to a switch buried way down in his stomach. You could never tell whether it was the machine or he. I guess when you dedicate yourself to something the way he has, you become something of a machine. You can't worry about your superficial responses. A year ago I gave him three thousand eight hundred dollars to write for a year. Now maybe he thinks he owes me something. I only gave him the money because I couldn't stand his accusing eye whenever I talked about writing. It was as if he were thinking he could do anything if he had my money. He wouldn't worry about a thing, just sit in his room and write. Three thousand eight hundred was a lot of money to him. It pressed a strong key in his stomach machine.

We crossed over the hill and Ornstein laughed. His eyes were shining and there was an easiness about him that I'd never seen before as he remembered the past, pointing out places where we used to play kick-the-can or ring-a-leerio in the caves behind the lookout point. He reminded me of the time in the cave when I had diarrhea from eating too many Sabrett's hot dogs with that slimy sauerkraut, and Brian, our Irish counselor, had sent him off to the candy store across the street to call my mother and have her pick me up. No one wanted to come near me.

"Would you like me to go see Jennifer and speak to her?" he asked.

"No, I don't need your help. Stop meddling in other people's private lives. Don't you have any private life of your own?"

Something seemed to stick in his throat.

"Are you two still messing around with junk? That's no good for you, Marcus. It was all right to smoke pot for a while, but that was college-boy stuff. Don't be a slave to some downtown junkie just because you can afford it. Do you want all of Max Rottner's hard-earned, tainted cash in the hands of some Wop connection on the lower East Side?"

I stopped for a second. I couldn't remember ever telling Ornstein about Larry Dolci. I had bought some pot for him while we were in college, but he had stopped smoking abruptly right after graduation, as if that were something you did as a kid, but now that you were out in the wide world, you were beyond that kind of stimulation. Was there a sixth sense about him?

"I've stopped narcotics," I said.

"As of when?"

"As of three days ago. I have no use for it anymore. Remember how you used to say that a man should be able to make himself high by his own thoughts and actions, without the aid of externals like drugs or liquor? Well that's what I've done. I'm higher than a kite."

"To coin a phrase."

"Yes, to coin a phrase."

"Let's run," said Ornstein as he took off at a canter around the bend in the path. "You can run now that you've licked junk."

"Who said I licked it? I'm just not taking it," I panted behind him.

"Maybe that girl wasn't so good for you after all; since she's been gone, you've found your old self again."

I stopped in my tracks. What did he mean by that? Did he know she was dead? At a moment like this my grandfather would have been master of the situation. No one, friend or foe, should be left knowing more than he should. And this social worker with a typewriter. ...But I had no gun. Ornstein was still stronger and faster than I. He was in the days of Stan Motion's Club and he still is. He stood there mocking me with his inner knowledge. Old Max would never have found himself alone in the hills of New York's biggest park with anyone—Van Cortland Park, V.C. Park, Ornstein had called it in honor of his heroes, the Viet Cong, who he hoped, someday, would be fighting a war of liberation in these very hills. He grinned as he told of them marching from the Park through the Bronx to Yankee Stadium. They would lie nights in the subways and in the early mornings terrorize the big-money interests centered in the Seagram's and Lever Brothers buildings. All the glass would shatter from the buildings as Park Avenue would become a pile of melting silicone from Fiftieth to Sixtieth Streets. I guess Ornstein is a true writer and likes to make up stories.

Someone has knocked on my door. Excuse me.

I sit on the floor stunned. Two hours have passed. I have hardly moved. When I interrupted myself, I went to the door. I uncovered the little window and saw Larry Dolci standing there with two of his cronies I did not recognize.

"Open up," he said, "or we'll send the police up to this apartment."

"I can't."

"What do you mean you can't?"

"It's stuck."

"How can a door be stuck?" he began to slam his fist against it. His friends did the same. They made a horrible din and I was afraid they would wake the whole floor. I opened the door.

"All right. Where is it?" said Dolci, bashing me against the wall. "Where do you keep it?"

He pulled out all the drawers he could find and threw them on the floor. I couldn't say anything. His friends, Mansueto and another hired hood, stood by the door and watched the corridor.

"Sing out!" he said again, this time grabbing me by the neck and tossing me onto the couch, which broke one of its antique legs. "A thin Jewish acquaintance of yours came to inform me you were through with drugs. Now, Marcus, I'm not that stupid. That never happens. You've found a new source. Who is it?"

I shook my head.

"Then let's have three grand as proof of good faith, little boy hip." His friends grinned. "Give us three grand and we'll leave you alone."

I'm not one to quarrel, particularly under the circumstances. I pulled out my checkbook and wrote him a check for three thousand dollars. Dolci then spit in my face.

"Trying to pull a fast one on us by stopping your check. How much cash do you keep here?"

"A few hundred."

"Give it."

I gave. Then they bound me up and locked me in the closet. I heard some furniture being thrown about. A few minutes later they were gone. They had not tied me up very carefully. I admit I was near tears when they were attacking me. Larry's two friends smiled then and I thought I heard them laughing at me as they closed the door on the way out. With the unwound end of a coat hanger, I unlatched the closet door. The house was a wreck. I have made no effort to fix it up. I am unable to do anything but sit in front of my type-

31

writer and pour it all out. I am only consoled that this is the kind of adventure that fills the life of a fugitive from justice. If Ornstein knew, he would be amazed. There I was the young, rich, ineffectual, ex-junkie quivering in the corner under the blows of my former master, the dope peddler. What a perfection in form. What shall I call myself? How about "Jersey Jewish"?

Somehow, amidst all their brutality, they never opened the harpsichord. Even the rudest of people with the most impoverished upbringings have an innate respect for beautiful antiques. My cherished Canaletto too remains intact. I remember once when I had a party over at my father's apartment a lot of downtown weirdos came over, but somehow they knew, without having been educated at all, that those paintings were worth something more than just money, and Dolci has his own peculiar brand of education. I'll write more of that party another time. For now I am tired. A game of ping-pong is still to be played, but I can see that my last two balls have been squashed under the foot of some oily Dago gangster. Nguyen Cao Ky was to have a rematch after yesterday's defeat by Ho Chi Minh. It is rumored, too, that Ngo Dinh Diem may rise from the dead, that is if the CIA permits it.

I must do something about removing the body. I need two blankets, one of which is a quilt, on top of my electric blanket in order to sleep at night. Imagine watching television with gloves on. I have been thinking of having the harpsichord removed. Perhaps some museum might be interested. That would be a big surprise. They could keep the harpsichord, body and all, in the Egyptian department of the Museum of Art, a kind of Baroque mummy.

Fourth Day...

I dreamt last night that Jennifer was still alive and we were living in a circus world with elephants and giraffes and clowns and cotton candy, but everybody was high on heroin. I wanted to talk to Jennifer but she was a trapeze artist and stood on the high wire—I guess it was Madison Square Garden—at the very center of the arena with a syringe in her hand. The spotlight was on her. The band played a crescendo of circus music as she raised the instrument to her arm, looking for a vein.

"No, no," I shouted. "You'll fall."

But the whole audience turned to me and told me to shush. Jennifer jabbed the needle into her vein, and just then all the animals that were in the cages in the ring below came out from behind the bars and started to dance in front of the barrier where the people were seated. I began to smile and the people in the audience began to smile, too, because the animals were so gentle and friendly, almost like animals in a cartoon, or more precisely like the pretty wooden animals on a merry-go-round. But then I raised my head and saw Jennifer hanging by her toe from the high wire. Her long hair fell beneath and the syringe dangled from her left hand. I realized that she was dead. The audience followed my gaze. I heard a gasp.

I woke up this morning with a new strong desire to tell somebody all that has happened. Ornstein was the likely candidate, for he must have known most of it already and I own $3,800 of his soul. But when I left the apartment, it was only a quarter to seven. My dreams would not let me sleep and it was clearly too cold to stay in bed.

I thought I might drive into Newark or Jersey City for some ping-pong balls, but I walked around the shopping center near my apartment until a J. J. Newberry store opened where I made my purchase and had some breakfast while reading the Newark and New York papers. Nassar was making trouble. The predicted turnout for the protest march today was smaller than usual because of the unrest in the Middle East. By then it was nearly eight-thirty and I entered the Fairlane and headed for the city. I parked near the fountain restaurant and walked over to the Central Park Mall to watch them set up the rostrum for the speakers at the Peace March. I went over hoping to see Ornstein among the men setting up. I sat down opposite the Mall thinking about Jennifer and how I wanted to tell someone about what happened to her. I wondered about the various New Jersey laws about the harboring of a dead body. With all those miracle operations in *Life* magazine, maybe something could be done. No, that's hoping for too much. That's ridiculous. I was surrounded by pigeons and I wore my frayed ski jacket. I must have looked like some punk kid and that's the way I like to look.

In a way it's fitting that Jennifer was the one to die from drugs, because she was the one to introduce us to them.

I hadn't realized the kind of friends she had been keeping when I started to date her in New York. She had this friend Yvonne, now a dancer, who always smoked marijuana. I hadn't known too many people like that before. I didn't know then that Jennifer regularly smoked it with her. I thought Jennifer was just a kid because she was a virgin when we met. Actually she used me as a can opener, I suppose, because the week after we first made love—that was two years ago September—she took off for three days to Fire Island with Henderson, the actor I wrote was in our crowd, who was then married to Lorraine. (She is now his girl friend.) She came back from Fire Island a changed person. She wore the thick mascara make-up of the Village chick and talked like she'd been making love since the age of four. She snubbed me for several months after that. I was an inexperienced child. I'd call her every night or two, but then I went away to college and was able to forget for a while. Even then I deluged her with letters, postcards, boxes of chocolate and surprise presents like sweaters and nylon hose. Most weekends I would drive to New York and call her up, seemingly on the spur of the moment, just to say hello, while trying to give the impression I was in town for a big date. She must have known because that Thanksgiving, when I was living at my stepfather's apartment while he was out of town, she appeared at the door stoned out of her mind. She told me she had been smoking pot with Yvonne and Henderson for five hours and she just wanted to see how I was making out with my date.

"That is, if you have a date...."

"Not this weekend."

"Then how'd you like to go out with me?"

"Sure, Jennifer. Why not?"

"Stop trying to act so casual. I know you come down to New York every weekend panting after me. Well, Jennifer knows her way around. You can ask Henderson and Shahib Lewis."

He was a Negro jazz composer.

"You think I'm gonna go out with a boy who doesn't know how to smoke boo?"

I went over and turned on the stereo, then offered her a drink. Suddenly she had an entire change of heart.

"I'm so lonely, Marcus. Take care of me. You understand my problems. You're like me."

She put her head on my shoulder and started to cry. I comforted her and then we made love. That night I smoked marijuana for the first time. I felt like I was entering into her secret world. I liked it very much and smoked some again the next morning. We woke up and rolled a joint before we even had orange juice or coffee and passed it back and forth between us. Pretty soon we didn't want to get out of bed. It was not sex that held us there, just our mutual stupor. I don't know if I ever had a morning like that before or since. There was something so beautiful about it, so close.

The marchers were beginning to assemble for the demonstration. They made me feel very old, very used up. All these fifteen-year-old girls who paint their faces, they scare me and make me think of Jennifer. Maybe I'm a part of a different generation or maybe not part of any generation at all. For all I've fooled with drugs, I've never tried LSD. I'm afraid. I never took drugs for any spiritual purpose. I took drugs because it was a hip thing to do, or because it put me out and made me forget things. Maybe these kids scare me because I hate crowds. They love to be together. They want to put their arms around each other. But I'd be afraid of body sweat or halitosis and if somebody put a flower in my hair I think, deep down, I'd feel like he was calling me a faggot.

I moved over to where the older people were standing. They all looked so respectable, like Queens College professors of anthropology with their wives and children. Crewcut architect types held infants over their heads. Some held placards with moderate statements: "Negotiate with the Viet Cong" or "No More Bombing of the North." A group of neo-Nazis assembled across the street with their greasy blond hair slicked back and nearly touching the collar of their motorcycle jackets. From behind me, I heard a chant: "Ungower, Black Power! Ungower, Black Power! Beep, beep. Bam, bam." An earnest-looking young man in a pea jacket handed me a mimeographed flyer. I wanted to bolt and run. It announced the principal speakers for the rally: Norman Thomas, Dr. Spock and Mrs. Martin Luther King. I looked again for Ornstein. I did not see him. The crowd was already too big to hope to find somebody. I felt myself being pushed forward. I brushed up against the speaker's platform itself. A sudden thought struck me.

"Excuse me," I said to a stooped, rumpled old man above me. "But have you seen Sigmund Ornstein? He's on the Steering Committee of the Students for a Democratic Society and I thought you might know where he was."

"No, I can't say that I do," said the man, as he turned the other way and began to shuffle through some papers he was carrying. I couldn't tell whether he knew Ornstein or not. He had such a kind face I was tempted to tell him the whole story without even knowing his name. I managed to speak Jennifer's name. Someone clapped me on the back and I heard a bellicose laugh from behind. Through the laugh, a fat newspaper cameraman was saying, "Do you know who you just asked for directions, boy? That was Dr. Spock. Do you known who Dr. Spock is, boy?"

"Yes, yes, I do." I wanted to insult him or buy him off, but I turned away. In the distance I saw some familiar faces camouflaged behind a morass of signs and paint. I thought I saw Lorraine, Henderson's girl friend, standing with some friends beneath a long ornate banner which read "This is the Hour of the Flower." Them, too. Lorraine came running toward me holding out a pair of prisms toward me.

"Marcus, did you see my new Tripster Glasses?" I shook my head. The others joined her and she continued, as if to announce my presence.

"Well, look who's here. Our man Marcus R. Didn't expect to see you on the march."

"I'm looking for somebody."

A girl on one end of the banner said: "You're not *the* Marcus R.? I've heard a lot about you, baby. You're my kind of cat. Free snow for everybody. Got any glassine envelopes on you, baby? It might mean a little action for you...."

"I'm looking for somebody."

"He's looking for his connection at the Peace March, isn't that wild?" continued the girl. "You meet and greet all your friends, rich and poor, hip and square, at the antiwar demonstrations."

"I'm looking for Sigmund Ornstein and he's nobody's conection. He lives mostly on wheat germ. Has anybody seen him?"

They all looked blank. It's easy to forget how few people actually know Ornstein. He hides so much behind his cloak of detachment he'll go for days without speaking to a soul.

Another girl broke into the conversation. She looked very nervous and held a tattered copy of *The Plague.* "Don't you think

36

we should cool this conversation? There may be reporters around us and we wouldn't want that kind of publicity for the demonstration. Let's all wait to turn on until after the show, huh?"

I began to back away from them, but stopped, remembering to pass on some last words to Lorraine. "I'm at a new address," I said. "Remember to tell Henderson. I'll give it to you sometime."

"Right, do that," she said, but she and the others had already started moving off in the other direction.

I sniffed myself to see if the last few days in my cold apartment had given me any particularly body odor. I couldn't tell. I began walking off to the park gate. Behind me a folk singer had already mounted the rostrum. The older crowd had joined hands and they were singing "We Shall Overcome." Another younger contingent was yelling "Hell, no, we ain't goin'." I turned and threaded my way back through the lines, looking for Ornstein in every face. They all swayed together and sang together as I wove up one file and down another. The people all looked alike and I worried about whether I could pick my friend out of the crowd, even if I passed him. I had to tell someone about Jennifer. Someone who would be understanding. He wasn't here. I broke through the file in front of me and then the one after that. I wanted to annoy protesters, but they only smiled at me as I pushed through their lines. I pushed harder, ran through file after file, but still they only smiled. I didn't want their flowers. I wanted to tell them that a murderer ran through their ranks, but I couldn't speak. Home, home. And phone Ornstein. He'll have to listen. He's in my debt.

I drove hurriedly back to the apartment, moved swiftly into an open elevator, reached my floor and pulled up short. The door was half open. My second cousin Selma stood in the living room with a tall, mustachioed fellow in a hopsack suit. They were both wearing green berets.

"This is Dr. Wasserman, Marcus," said Selma.

"Some party you had here last night," he said, trying to be affable. "Something must have gone wrong with your air conditioner. We fixed it for you."

"So I see."

They did a double-take as I walked back over to the window and turned the Fedders on again.

"Where'd you get those silly hats?" I asked. "You must have been to some party yourselves."

"You know about Mr. Schlicht's new business, Marcus," the psychiatrist—it didn't take me long to figure out what kind of a doctor he was—broke in before Selma could explain herself. She was almost naked without her PR uniform, that floppy red hat.

"Don't you think it's rather ingenious of him?" Wasserman continued. "Sit down, Marcus. You seem all jittery."

"It's because I've got a corpse stashed in this apartment."

"That's nice—boy or girl?"

"Girl. A sweet young thing."

Selma looked furious. She was about to hit me with her handbag.

"That's all right, Selma," the psychiatrist broke in again. "I can take care of this. I'm used to this kind of thing....Why do you feel hostile toward me, Marcus?"

"It's my girl friend's body. She's been dead for almost four days now. I've hidden her in the harpsichord. That's why I turned the air conditioner up. Preserve the body. I gave her an overdose of narcotics."

"Very amusing," he said, wrapping his hand on top of the instrument. "But don't you realize it's an antique?"

"Yes, that's just why I hid her there. I didn't think anybody would think of it."

"Particularly since the mechanism inside a harpsichord would not allow room for a bread box, much less a body?" queried Wasserman.

"I took it all out and dismantled the equipment. It all went out in the garbage. And Jennifer is a small girl. She wears junior petite clothes."

He looked more closely at the harpsichord for a split second.

"And then you nailed it down, front and back, I suppose?"

I nodded.

"But there I've trapped you." He removed his glasses and bared his teeth. "Valuable harpsichords such as this one are always nailed down for protection. You need only check at the Museum of Art, or at the Frick."

"Have you ever seen such a one in a private home before, Dr.—?"

"Dr. Wasserman."

"Dr. Wasserman?"

The psychiatrist tilted his head toward Selma who was seated on the couch with a most disturbed look on her face. She had

38

replaced her floppy red hat on her head and was in the process of securing the green beret in her purse. She looked up.

"I don't know why I want to help you, Marcus. Sergei is one of the finest psychiatrists in New York or in the world for that matter. He doesn't want to mold you into some kind of docile, conforming ant. He's not that way himself. And he's only come all the way out to Jersey as a favor to me, Marcus."

The doctor—Sergei, I should say—paced slowly about the room and into the bedroom. He eyed everything suspiciously, playing the role of an emotional Sherlock Holmes.

"Everything is, shall we say, rather helter-skelter."

"Some dope peddlers were here last night to rough me up. A shakedown." I had lost interest in telling him what had happened, or rather, in the process of telling him, the desire had overtaken itself and been quelled. The best way to prevent him from investigating the facts further would be to go on with the truth.

"You like to live in disorder, Marcus? It's the sign of a chaotic mind, you know." And then, tilting once more toward Selma, "but, as Dostoyevsky has said, 'Disorder is often the hidden search for beauty.'"

With all his talk of beauty, I noticed Dr. Wasserman physically for the first time. I noted before that he was tall and mustachioed and wore a hopsack suit, but these were only first impressions. I realized now that he was a man of tremendous physical presence. He was not a pound overweight, but he loomed over you like a man twice his breadth. His temples were flecked with gray and he had that air of distinction so highly prized that certain men's clothing companies are willing to pay the price of Cesar Romero or perhaps even Gregory Peck. He might have been Peck himself had I known that he was not an actor but a psyhchiatrist.

"Please be in my office the day after tomorrow at eleven o'clock. I'm going to have to be harsh with you, Marcus." Selma nodded her head in approval. "No one's ever told you the truth about yourself. Your parents have been afraid to talk to you for a long time. Perhaps they feel they've failed you, because of their divorce or some other reason. Whatever it is, we'll get to the root of it. You want to get to the root of it, don't you, Marcus?"

I nodded. I was tired.

"For example, when you make up a story like that one, you have a reason for inventing the fiction you chose. You were trying to express some inner fear or aggression."

Dr. Wasserman took the beret off his head and started to chuckle.

"Funny for a grown man to wear one of these, isn't it? And I bet you're against that war, aren't you?"

"I'm indifferent," I said.

Dr. Wasserman nodded and turned the front door handle, mumbling about my eleven o'clock appointment. Selma led him out the door, but while it was still a crack open I heard her call back something about remembering to clean up the apartment. I decided to call a maid. That is certainly what Grandfather Max would have done in such a situation. He might have called two, but I by-passed that idea because I did not feel like explaining twice about the faulty air-conditioning and about how fragile the harpsichord was and how it was not to be moved or opened. I do, I hasten to add, have a regular girl who comes in once a week, twice when there's a party, to clean the apartment; she is not due for two days.

As far as I know, and I assume it is the truth, Max never engaged in underhanded dealings directly. He didn't like to hear when the rules were being altered slightly and excessive pressure was being applied. He would turn away from his assistant, Tubal.

"Tubal," he would say, "I can't hear you."

He had a tremendous feeling for people. He knew what someone was trying to say long before they said it. He used this knowledge to keep his hands clean. The police had his house under surveillance for several years before he was apprehended, and then it was on the perjury charge. The police out front didn't even know he was arrested.

Max was not what would be described today as intelligent. People wouldn't even say he had a lot of common sense, but he knew what he had to do. He knew, for example, that he had to go to college to make the appropriate business ties well before he learned to speak English. He had a friend from the old country translate *The Wall Street Journal* for him. Like many robber barons, he had a passionate loyalty toward members of his family and a few close friends. But would you really call him a robber baron? He was more of a fireball of ambition, a little dynamo, a Napoleon. A master of wrestling, collegiate or Greco-Roman, boxing and all manner of self-defense. He was a fanatic about physical exercise and fitness—and above all, a rigidly religious man. His father was a rabbi and either out of fear of disrupting his honored ghost or out of some natural propensity toward the devout, Max would rise early each day for the morning prayer, carefully placing the phylacteries and tifilin, and excuse the moral violence he had committed the previous day in the name of Mammon.

Of all the things that I have done, I think the one that would disturb Grandfather Max the most would be that Jennifer was a gentile.

That never bothered my mother or any of his children. Quite the contrary. They are very determined assimilationists and they were all very pleased when they heard I was going with a girl from a prominent Christian family. And this from a family whose combined wealth outstripped that of the combined wealth of the Da Silvas by a thousandfold, or even more. What my mother must have liked was that Jennifer's great-grandfather was some bigwig in the Confederacy. One of my uncles in Los Angeles and Selma gave generously to two civil rights organizations, but they would have jumped at the chance to join the United Daughters of the Confederacy. Anything with over ten years status attracted them. Of course they all changed their tune about Jennifer's family once they found out what she was like. It only confirmed their opinion of the decadence of the Southern tradition. They're all immoral perverts. Just like any Tennessee Williams play.

I can't tell you how my mind has cleared since I made my confession to Dr. Wasserman. Psychiatrists do have a value, except they rarely realize when their work is being most successful. There is a new freedom in knowing that, although the truth of a situation is incriminating, the truth will never be believed and therefore is powerless to incriminate you. As long as I choose the right time and the right tone of voice, I can tell the whole world about what I have done and still remain above suspicion. It is true that ciminals always return to the scene of the crime, only there is a difference in the method of conveyance they use for their return. Some return in a black coat in the middle of the night, trying to erase all the fingerprints and make sure that no evidence was left behind. They are apprehended immediately. Others appear

41

in a red plaid sports jacket, proclaiming that they are guilty. If they are obvious criminal types with a likely story, they will often be written off as insane and placed in a mental institution, surely, dare you contradict me, not a bad fate for a man who is guilty of a homicide. If, on the other hand, and I place myself in this group, you have no criminal record, no crime has been reported, you have a reputation for slight, though in no ways drastic, instability, you tell people you have committed a highly outlandish, even morally repulsive crime, and they pay no attention to you at all. They want to get on to other things.

Now all that stands in the way of my new freedom is the *corpus delecti*, as they say in Erle Stanley Gardner novels. Shahib Lewis knows some people in Harlem, so I think I'll call him and casually engage him in conversation about how to remove a dead body. Meanwhile, I want to return to my former habits. I might even blow a little pot, but I think I'll stay away from smack for a while. Also, I haven't read the *Daily News* in four days. How will I know what's going on in the world? I miss Charlie McHarry, not to mention the Voice of the People. There is nothing more inspiring than a good reactionary *Daily News* editorial when you're looking for a fun way to pass a slow afternoon. If I go onto the street now, I should just be able to pick up a morning edition. Tomorrow I begin Operation Removal. Tonight I might as well relax and enjoy myself. I have a new box of ping-pong balls and there's a rematch waiting to be played. Tonight perhaps I shall support the National Liberation Front, at least for a while.

Fifth Day...

The same dream repeated again and again throughout the night. Circus. Circus. Read a book once called *The Circus of Dr. Lao*. Kind of like that. Strange animals out of the past. Mixture of real and fantastic. Dinosaurs and unicorns. I screamed. Jennifer would fall but she hanged by her toe from the wire, never seeming to move. Ornstein was the ring master. He knew all the animals. They ate from the palm of his hand. Technicolor dream with large production numbers like 1930's Hollywood musicals. One was a Venetian fantasy. Scantily clad Italian girls with bandannas around their necks climbed a hundred ropes simultaneously to "O Solo Mio" while an equal number of gondoliers held the ropse from the bottom so they wouldn't shake too much. Grandfather Max wandered among them dressed in a Jewish gabardine saying, "There is no force in the decrees of Venice. I stand for judgment. Answer—shall I have it?"

My sheets soaked through with sweat. I awoke trembling, cold. Ran to Ornstein's apartment, but first called Shahib Lewis. He said the best way to dispose was to drive body upstate New York and dump in Hudson, isolated spot, weighted down with stones. He wanted to know why I asked. Hung up. Drove to Ornstein's. Pulled him out of bed. Not yet eight o'clock. Had chills. Told him I was frightened. Told him everything. He said tell police. It was an accident. But it wasn't an accident. The moment before I plunged the needle in her arm I thought: What if this time she arches her back like a dying animal and goes stiff? We all think that, Ornstein would have said, but I didn't tell him. I told him what he used to say in college: Superior people are above the law. If there is a morality, theirs should not be governed by outside forces. They must learn to punish themselves. I told him how I planned to remove the body. Wouldn't he come? He said yes. Don't leave apartment, but I left it.

I must have written that last paragraph in a delirium. After I left Ornstein's apartment, I was supposed to go directly home. He was going to tidy up, fastidious young man that he is, and then follow me. Instead, I took the subway downtown to Larry Dolci's and bought ten decks of heroin. I had no intention of using it, but my life had revolved so closely around drugs that I literally have no idea about what to do with my time. Also, now that the room has been cleaned and the corpus delecti is about to be removed, with luck I can return to my normal life. I enjoy playing the host and most of my friends use smack a great deal more frequently than I. I must clarify one thing: I did not write that last paragraph on drugs. I was merely upset about the kind of sleep I've been getting. Perhaps, later on, I shall try to write a few words on dope, but, after all, that kind of thing's been done an awful lot lately. I wouldn't want to be accused of being a slave of fashion. I guess you might say I have a certain kinship to William Burroughs, though. He's the only junkie I know who shares my wealthy background and writes. He's Burroughs Business Machines, you know. But I doubt that he ever killed off any of his girl or boy friends with an O.D.

I bought a special tool for removing nails on my way home and have pulled them out of the harpsichord with hardly a trace. I have not opened it yet, but there is no need for that. I shall follow the example of my grandfather and not put my foot in any deeper than necessary. He always went forward step by step. First into college, then into the right fraternity, the only one, the only Jewish one, of course. There he made the life-long business connections that kept him out of the hands of the law for so long: a federal judge, an economist, a newspaper columnist for *The Wall Street Journal*. None of these men had yet achieved the status they were to attain, but Max was, as I have said, a good judge of character. He was the president of the fraternity. They were all short men and very clannish and Max was the shortest and most loyal. He never crossed his family and he never crossed any of those men. They were like family. I remember having to call them "Uncle" when I was a little boy and being disconcerted since they were not blood relatives. Do not be misled. None of these men were criminals or even slightly shady public figures, a minor miracle in New York, but they remained faithful to Max through all his shady dealings. After all, he was the president of the fraternity. For him, and for him alone, they would ignore individual or public morality.

Ornstein's face was all concern when he arrived at my apartment. The internal sympathy keys were depressed. He said nothing, walked right to the harpsichord and peerd in. I think he was trying to verify my story as quickly as possible.

"How are we going to get her out of here?" he asked.

"I'll have them bring my car around; we'll put her in the trunk and cross the Tappan Zee into New York and head upstate."

"You realize you're making me an accessory. Don't you think it would be better for you to call the police? How do you think you'll be able to carry the body out to the car in broad daylight?"

I couldn't answer both questions at once, so I didn't try. I was thinking how good it would be for the temperature in the apartment to return to normal. The outdoor temperature had risen into the high fifties and the body was beginning to give off a pungent smell. There's something about these fashionable apartment houses that doesn't mix well with the odor of decaying flesh.

The harpsichord was completely opened up.

"Grab an end," I said to Ornstein, pointing at the enshrouded body within.

He was taken aback by my new commanding voice. What does he know of the behavior of the murderer? He does not realize that we have nothing to lose.

"Grab an end," I repeated, this time even more authoritatively than before.

I noticed a nervous tic in Ornstein's shoulder which I hadn't seen since we were children. He lifted his end and together we raised Jennifer gently from the harpsichord and placed her on the floor. Ornstein noticed the glassine packets of heroin on the table and said nothing. I don't know if he knew what they were, but I suppose he could have guessed.

I just wanted to take the corpse right out to the car without stopping, but Ornstein took excessive precautions. We moved down the back stairs landing by landing. Each time he ran ahead for a hundred steps, then up again. Jennifer would rest head first on the stairs. Ornstein was carrying her head end. I was beginning to perspire by the time we reached the seventh floor and we were both drenched in sweat as the large door on the second floor came into view. I told Ornstein to wait with the body while I drove the car around. He cursed me for not having had it there before as I ran off. The Ford was parked in the cellar garage of the building. I drove it up the ramp and alongside the delivery entrance. The back door was locked and I rang four times.

"Who is it?" cried Ornstein in a disguised voice.

"Forest Dale Cemeteries, delivery service," I replied and he opened the door.

"What a comedy of errors," he said and I nodded.

I opened the trunk swiftly; we transported the body from within. The service entrance locked once more behind us. I slammed the trunk. We checked our trail to the door for drops of blood or other evidence, but how could there be any blood when there was no wound? Ornstein sniffed about as if making a last test for some minute implicating clue. He was beginning to enjoy the role of fugitive. I felt like Mephistopheles tempting Faust away from the narrow path. I had never been able to do it with drugs. I was becoming intoxicated by the new shift in the balance of power in our relationship.

"I won't be needing you any more," I told Ornstein. "You're in this deep enough as is." He stood there blankly looking at me.

"I still think you should report her death to the police. After all, it was an accident."

"I'm not so sure," I said, slamming the door of the car behind me. "You have all the money you need, don't you?"

I peeled off toward the George Washington, crossed it and headed straight on the Cross Bronx Expressway. Something drove me east and I headed for the Whitestone Bridge and onto the Island. There was a slight engine knock in the Fairlane. It is pale blue with spinners. I was wearing my ski parka. I realized what I was doing. I was unconsciously heading for Martha Da Silva's place in East Hampton, on the Southern Parkway, speeding by the various "meres" and "necks" and "bays." How appropriate to send Jennifer to her watery grave here at her ancestral home, to be washed up, faceless and mysterious, on some starry night at Montauk. But this wasn't, of course, her ancestral home. That was down in Selma, Alabama, or Albany, Georgia, or maybe even Jackson, Mississippi. I eyed myself proudly in the rear-view mirror as the car passed the Long Island windmill. I stopped about a block from Aunt Martha's house. I didn't want to be seen. That might remind her of her niece and she might call me and a whole series of complications might be set off.

Instead I sat there wondering why I didn't feel guilty about Jennifer's death. Someone or something must be to blame. We have a variety of choices. We have my parents and Jennifer's parents. They certainly did not fulfill their tasks. Then we have Jennifer. And we have society. And of course, there's always me. I did perform the fatal act and I have reached my majority. Or we could say that it was a combination of these factors. But that's the oldest cop-out in the world. Or then we could say that no one is to blame. But that's the second oldest cop-out. Or then there's salvation in faith. But sometimes I think that, for all the wise men say about the many levels of the Bible, religion was invented to quiet us down and gives us simple answers to the most complex questions. And what bothers me most is that the crime was an accident, and perhaps I am only as blameworthy as others who have an accident. What is to distinguish between accidents? Did I do any more than slip on a banana peel when I killed my girl friend?

I remembered Shahib Lewis' instructions. Drop the body in the Hudson. Is that river a special elixir for corpses? Quickly I changed

46

my course and took the Long Island ferry to Bridgeport. But now it was late afternoon and a new harmony welled within me as I sped south on the Connecticut Turnpike toward the Cross Westchester Expressway.

Psychiatrists have always failed me, but long drives have replaced them. The Ford is my most reliable comforter and my only one, now that Jennifer is gone. I never had to strain to keep its attention, just turn the ignition. With Jennifer, even after that Thanksgiving when she came to me of her own free will, it was a perpetual fight. I'm not trying to blame her, not saying that a woman led me on the path of iniquity, certainly the roots had to be there. But I went further and further into the labyrinth of the amoral or the immoral in her pursuit.

That first morning we lolled around in bed smoking marijuana. I thought of nothing. We just enjoyed the sensation of tickling each other or the delicious rubbing of fine percale sheets between our legs. After a while, I fell back to sleep. The Cannabis must have had strong depressant powers. (It never did later.) When I awoke, Jennifer was gone. I didn't see her for the next couple of weeks and when I called her house she was either out or in too much of a hurry to speak. Then, just before my Christmas vacation, I thought of an idea, called her house, got her on the phone for "just a second," but, before she could say anything, spoke:

"Listen, Jennifer, I've just bought two hundred dollars worth of Moroccan hashish and I wonder if you might want to come over next Friday and smoke a little."

"Where'd you get that?" she asked.

"A friend of mine returned from North Africa by freighter with a large shipment of the best money can buy. He called me because he knows my reputation and knows I can afford the best."

"Who's this?"

"A friend of mine I said. A jazz musician. A Negro."

"I didn't know you knew any jazz musicians."

"You don't know all there is to know about me, Jennifer."

I smile now remembering the satisfaction of uttering those words. For the first time in our relationship, except when I had bought her the birthday cake, did I feel confident of myself. I knew that somehow I could obtain two hundred dollars worth of hashish, although I had no idea how those things were done. I didn't know any jazz musicians either, but I had heard the music and I knew that when they said jazz they didn't mean the Dukes

47

of Dixieland or Al Hirt or even Dave Brubeck. I looked in the Manhattan directory for a Shahib Lewis. Jennifer had mentioned him and I knew he had access to all kinds of drugs. Remembering my grandfather, I recalled that money could move mountains where something shady was involved. Grandfather Max used to say that in New York the mountain comes to any Mohammed with a fifty-dollar bill. A corny truth. There was no Shahib Lewis in the directory, nor had information the listing of any such name. I looked once more at the gargantuan list of Manhattan Lewises. I knew that he lived in Harlem. Quickly springing to my eye was a Samuel Lewis on 128th Street. From Samuel to Shahib was one easy step. I called Samuel. Three rings and then someone answered.

"May I please speak to Shahib Lewis?"

"You want HO 3-5373. That's my cousin Miles Lewis."

I disconnected quickly and rang the new number.

"Shahib Lewis?"

"Speaking."

"I'm a friend of Jennifer Da Silva."

"Of Jennifer's?"

"Yes...I was wondering if you could sell me two hundred dollars worth of pot."

I heard a big horse laugh on the other end. I realized that I was bold and obvious in my request, but I had nothing whatever to say to him besides this.

"I think we can arrange it. Come to my apartment tonight."

"I'm calling you from three hundred miles away."

"This is a seller's market, baby. And I'm making my sale tonight. Be here tonight. The big house opposite the diamond shop. Third floor. I'll be looking forward to meeting you. Any friend of Jennifer's is a friend of mine, as they say."

I caught a plane to New York and was at Shahib Lewis' apartment in three hours. He was very short and thin and wore blue sunglasses with tight pants and a black button down shirt open at the collar. I felt better when I saw him because on the plane I had been imagining one of those six-eight Fruit of Islam types with shaven heads we see in *Life* magazine. Lewis had a high voice and was soft-spoken. He led me up the stairs into his apartment. The building wasn't a Harlem tenement, but rather lower middle class, the kind you associate with Bronx Jewish-Italian neighborhoods. There were no sweaty fat ladies in the halls. Only one crying child could be heard through a closed door, and there was no smell of urine or garbage. Lewis' apartment was one big room with a kitchenette and bath. Japanese *goa* mats were spread out across the floor. Two large abstract paintings covered the far wall and a baby grand piano stood in the corner. Lewis said he was a jazz composer-arranger. The last of a reefer glowed in the ashtray on the coffee table. I still would have called it a reefer in those days. Today I'd say a "roach" for the end of a marijuana cigarette, though even that term is going out of fashion. Next to the ashtray I saw my first syringe, first extra-legal syringe anyway. Lewis saw my expression and began to smirk. I must have panicked because he came over and clapped me on the back, told me not to worry. He went over to the piano and started to play some chords. He was very good, but tired quickly of his playing, walked to the icebox and offered me a beer. I wanted very much to ask him for my purchase, but hesitated fearing I would break some special protocol. Lewis sat down beside me, rose again to play a chord on the piano, and abruptly sat down and looked at me.

"My sister stayed in Mississippi," he said. "She was with the Mississippi Summer Project and she decided to stay on and help in the movement. We're very proud of her. She's a high school teacher in Brooklyn, the Brownsville area."

He stared at me very intensely and I couldn't tell whether he was putting me on.

"Is she older or younger?" I asked.

"Who?" His mind was on something else.

"Your sister."

"She's my twin."

"Do you have a large family?"

Shahib turned suddenly into a short, black furor.

"What do you think this is, Park Avenue social hour? You came here to buy some pot, rich boy. It will cost you a hundred dollars. I don't know how you got my name but I'm no connection, I'm a composer. You all think you can come up to Harlem, purchase your little illicit pleasure and disappear unmarked. It used to be whores; now it's drugs. Well, I had to pay my dues to go out and buy that pot for you, so I'm entitled to a commission, one hundred dollars extra."

I took out my wallet and counted him out three hundred and twenty-five dollars, twenty-five more than his already overpriced three hundred. He took off his sunglasses for the first time and stared at me for several minutes. First he shut one eye and looked at me, then he shut the other. The way his eye rolled over my features, he looked like the first mate on a whaling ship sizing up a new harpooner recruit. And then, just as in the movies the old hand decides the new recruit is all right after all, he pushed a jar of cookies over to me.

"Peyote," he said. "It's not worth twenty-five dollars, but it builds strong bones."

"I thought peyote was a cactus."

"You grind it up in a meat grinder until it becomes a green paste and then you bake it in the oven like any other cookie. It's much better than eating the cactus raw. You don't get sick to your stomach. If you don't eat four of those cookies, you won't feel anything."

I nodded.

I didn't like the idea that I was eating alone as he sat there and watched me. The cookies had a bland taste and he held his beer out to me to help get them down. Not long thereafter I began to hallucinate for the first time in my life. I found myself alone on the streets of Harlem. Dark faces strolled past me and their skin seemed to flow. A human face would dissolve into a street lamp and ooze out again, a viscous material. It was that twilight hour in New York and the lights had just come on to compete with a gray winter sunset. I was wandering aimlessly for the first time in my life, unafraid in Harlem. I passed a storefront church and rhythm and blues bar. Across was the Harlem Rentakar Service and I decided I would rent a car and go visit Jennifer. Only in Harlem would they rent to someone in my condition. I can't even remember signing the rental papers. Marcus Rottner was six different human beings to me.

I drove a Cadillac sedan to East Hampton at commuter time, the same road I drove while recalling this story, and when I arrived at Jennifer's aunt's, they thought I had been drinking. When I told Jennifer it was peyote, she got all excited and wanted to make love. But when we arrived at a Howard Johnson's Motor Inn, I told her I couldn't possibly make love in my condition, and this excited her even more, but in a different way. The next morning I realized Shahib Lewis had never given me the marijuana I had paid for, but I didn't want Jennifer to know anything, so I never called. Besides, she was high on goof balls and very hard to get along with.

If I were a moralist now, I could point my finger and shake my head. I was driving along with that young girl, once high on goof balls, dead in my back trunk. Let that be a lesson to all of you! But something like this happens in New York every day. People are violent and escapist. The stories that once drew oo and aah from our grandmothers wouldn't turn our heads anymore. What's another death, another murder, another rape? And need we complain about it? It's the natural state of things in our world. I am beginning to understand why I am so fascinated by my grandfather. I want to change places with him. He comes from the time when New York was an Earthly Paradise. Bootleggers and racketeers may have ruled the world. But at least we were able to deal with them. They killed within a frame, not totally irrationally. Even though I may have murdered Jennifer by accident, and even though she is the only one I have ever killed, I am much more dangerous than my grandfather's friends ever were. Even my parents, because they are alive today, forty years after the so-called lawless era of Prohibition, must perforce have more violence in their hearts than Max. When and if Jennifer is discovered and I am apprehended, they will cluck and pity and rationalize about the recent family disgrace. In the end, however, they're all as bad as I am, at least I suppose they are.

Fears were simple in Grandpa Max's day. People used to say, "Your grandfather was a very complex man." But they were wrong. He was very simple. He first went to school because he was afraid of being a shoe-shine boy. Then when he got to college everybody was in the process of baking a big, fat juicy pie called America—and he wanted a slice. Who wouldn't? He even wanted a big slice, maybe the biggest. Why not? Call it asserting his masculinity. Call it self-justification of a short man, a Napoleon complex. Call it what you will. That's only a motivation and motivations come cheap. Only I envy my grandfather because he was a man of iron, he had a will. He said "yes" to the world in a negative sense. Only all the time he was trying to get rid of his Jewish gabardine. Tubal, his partner (they cleaned up the Perrin Beer account together in Brooklyn), couldn't help him. Even when he wore a cutaway coat and handmade silk shirts from Sulka's, nothing could help him, the gabardine clung to his underskin. His childen were Jessica's denying what their father had done, denying that he even existed. My Uncle Herman gives a hundred thousand dollars a year to mental health in Southern California, hoping and praying that the money will assuage their collective guilt in some mysterious way. They are trying to pay back the pound of flesh exacted by their father, but the protoplasm oozes through their fingers. The old man always had so much more style than Jessica. She was a kind of an insipid young Jewess.

I continued driving down by the Hudson River edge, trying to decide where I should deposit the corpus delecti. I wanted to leave Jennifer's corpse on the lawn of an old Dutch estate or float her on an air mattress moored in the Hudson just in front of their property, a modern Guinevere. Here lies a maid, it would say, that many a knight fought over with crossed syringe to destroy the dragon within us. It was getting dark and the sun was setting over the river. I swallowed an amphetamine and continued my drive North. The red and white lights of the Rip Van Winkle were stretched out before me. When I was a little boy, this would have made me very excited, but now I grew very sad. I wanted to drive Jennifer in to the deep North and deliver her into the crevice of a frozen god. But I turned onto the bridge, stopping again to drop the body over. I was just opening the trunk when three motor-cycles drove up. Three Hell's Angels got off massive BMW's. Two of them wore black leather jackets and they had maroon cycles. The third wore a silk jacket and a helmet. He drove a black cycle with a cross. He was the leader and spoke for all of them.

"Gonna jump?" asked the leader. "Cause if you're gonna jump, we're gonna watch. We've seen four or five from here since sum-mer. Popular spot for nuts."

I made sure the trunk was locked tight.

"What's the matter? Not a talker? Listen, friend. If you're gonna jump, you might as well leave us your wallet. No sense in wasting hard-earned cash on the fishes."

His cronies picked their teeth menacingly. I could tell by the dilation of their pupils that they were high on something. I guessed it was horse.

"I don't want to jump. I was just getting a sandwich out of the trunk, but if you'd each like a fifty-dollar bill, I think I can spare it."

"This guy's some kind of joker," said the leader and the friend to the left lifted his left leg over the bike. A cluster of red rhinestones in the shape of a heart glistened on his shoe in the light of a passing truck. A gibbous moon had risen over the Hudson. Very poetic. The leader had a scar over his left eye. Hastily I pulled a crisp hundred and a fifty out of my wallet.

"You'll have to get change for yourselves." The leader snatched the bills from my hand with a look of purest suspicion. When I was about thirteen, there was a fairly rich kid who lived up Park Avenue from us. Once he had a party and kept throwing ten-dollar bills out the window hoping that some of his friends would dash frantically out of the apartment after them. But nobody did. We all thought they were counterfeit. We learned the truth on the way home when one of us discovered a newly minted ten under an automobile tire and had it validated at a bank. The next week I tried the same trick at a party and started to feel sick to my stomach.

A police car pulled up, siren on. The motorcyclists looked panicked. I appraised the situation quickly and realized I had nothing to fear. The policeman jumped out of the car ready to kill.

"These men just stopped to help me start my car. I stalled out here and they got it started for me."

The red light flashed on and off behind him and in that light the policeman was hard to separate from the Hell's Angels. For a moment I thought they were all together. The cop was wearing a leather winter jacket and was the exact same height as the others. Instinctively I reached for my wallet but stopped myself, wondering how he would take to a financial offering. I ran to the car and locked the door behind me. I expected to hear the roar of a siren behind me, but heard nothing. I turned off onto the first small road after the bridge, floored the accelerator and made several hairpin turns around dark corners trying to shake my pursuer. Pretty soon I was lost in the Catskills. I was farily sure I had eluded the police, but everytime I saw automobile headlights rounding a corner, I did my best to avoid them. Twice I backed the Ford into a driveway and turned out the lights movie fashion until the other car passed by. I began to believe that the FBI or Interpol were driving out in search of me. The dexedrine spansule was keeping me wide-awake. I found the blue signs leading to the New York Thruway and followed them for several miles.

The car trapped a deer and fawn in its high beam. The young animal froze in fear next to its mother. Their eyes glowed red in the bright beam. I stopped the car and got out. I wanted to give them some money, reaching for my wallet, but thought it silly. Then I thought to leave them Jennifer's body as an offering in exchange for all the deer killed by man, but I heard a car coming, jumped back behind the wheel and headed at top speed for the

Thruway, not even looking in the rear-view mirror. I got on at the Catskill entrance and headed south going eighty. An hour later I reached the final Thruway toll and dropped fifty cents into the exact change lane. The machine whirred and a siren went up. Two state troopers emerged simultaneously from opposite sides of the road. Either they were after me or someone had tried to run the toll gate. One of the cars was on my trail. The trooper signaled me over. I stopped and he came over to my car.

"Excuse me," he said. "But you didn't by some chance forget to put fifty cents in the meter?"

"No, I didn't. I just put a half dollar in."

"Our automatic call system indicates no payment."

"I believe I paid."

"Many people who drive through think they paid, but really haven't. It's a common mistake."

"Well, then, here's another fifty cents, although I still think I paid."

"I wish you wouldn't be so obstinate, sir. May I see your license and registration?"

I opened the glove compartment and started shuffling about for my license and registration. I found the registration, but no license.

"I guess I left my license at home."

"Then how can I be sure that you're a legal driver, sir? You are placing me in a compromising situation."

"Can't you call the New Jersey Department of Motor Vehicles? They must have a record of my license. The address is the same as on the registration."

A bead of sweat rolled down from the top of my forehead, onto my eyebrow and then splashed down onto my cheek.

"The Department of Motor Vehicles is closed at this hour, sir. What would you like me to do? We can't have people running around loose on the roads without a license to drive. It would be unfair to all those who have been properly trained. I'm afraid I'm going to have to detain you here until morning, Mr. Rottner."

"Suppose I were willing to pay another fifty cents?"

"But that would be impossible, sir. You haven't paid your first fifty."

"I will pay ten dollars to the toll booth here, and now just let me go home."

"What's your name?"

"Marcus Rottner. It says so on the registration."

"How can I be sure that's not a forgery. . . . Where'd you get this car?"

"It's my car. It was a present from my mother."

"Some present. Aren't you old enough to buy your own cars? Where do you live?"

"I live in New Jersey, but the address on the registration is on Park Avenue. I've moved since—"

"You're trying to tell me that you've got an incorrect address on here. That's a traffic violation far beyond speeding or running a light. It's the same thing as stealing a car. What'd you say your name was?"

The trooper was leaning far into the window of my car. The faint odor of ozone penetrated from between his teeth, which were a tobacco yellow. A huge Beacon Movers truck blinked green and red, roaring past us. The trooper stepped back and put his hand to his holster.

"You can go now," he said. "Just watch your step. Those toll booths are put there by the government of this state for your protection."

Once more I returned Jennifer within the limits of the State of New Jersey. She used to say that the only pure air was in Jersey, and that those noxious fumes would make you live a long life. You took in all possible bacteria just in the air you breathed. You built antibodies for everything. I guess that's why we liked Venice so much. The air there is polluted like Hoboken and Secaucus. When the tourist arrives in Venice, his immediate inclination is to leave because of the horrid stench. New York's garment district is also like Venice. The Negroes and Puerto Ricans are like gondoliers ferrying about gondolas of women's lingerie from the factory to the outlet store. The by-ways are like the streets and bridges of Venice. Business is done there as men barter and argue their goods. Max set up his first enterprise in that neighborhood, although it was just an investment counseling of sorts and not anything to do with clothing. I remember once, I imagine it was in a dream, I heard him fighting with another man on Thirty-fourth Street saying: "In the Rialto you have rated me about my moneys and my usances. Still have I borne it with a patient shrug. For sufferance is the badge of all our tribe. You call me misbeliever, cutthroat dog. And spit upon my Jewish gabardine. And all for use of that which is mine own."

Jennifer used to make fun of my love for my grandfather. She would say I was like a Chinese ancestor worshiper. One day she made me show her a picture of him. I never wanted to, because the only one I have is one of him dressed in the old country style. She wanted to know why he was dressed so peculiarly and why he was so short. She even thought he was a midget. When I told her that was how Jews used to dress, she began to laugh and hug me again and call me her Oriental, but from that day on, I would look occasionally in the mirror for some evidence of inscrutability. Maybe Max was a junkie before he came to this country, crouched on his haunches in some East European opium den, but he never drank, never even smoked, so I don't think that was too likely. It's funny that he never drank, since his first enterprising step out of the investment counseling business was providing calling cards and surreptitious publicity for speakeasies. Tubal and his assistants would do all the negotiating with the speaks. Max would arrive several days later (by this time he had graduated from his Jewish gabardine into a kind of George Raft outfit), never even mention a business connection, and eat a sumptuous gourmet meal. I found a desk in an attic of one of the old family country houses filled with these cards. He would drink no more than a small glass of wine, the finest vintage in the house.

Jennifer always would laugh when I told her about Max. She used to say I should raid his grave some night and disinter his spine and put it in place of mine. Once, when we were high, she made me put on a zoot suit and pretend I had a machine gun and ratatat everything in sight. Then she led me uptown to Shahib's apartment and spread herself out voluptuously on his sofa, saying she was a moll for Dutch Schultz's gang. It was a Sunday afternoon in early spring about one month ago. She began to take her clothes off, slowly, like a strip-tease artist. Shahib moved in on her and they began to make love before my eyes. There was nothing I could do. I stood watching, my pupils dilating and those little fuzzy dots running across the cornea which precede a vicious headache. When Jennifer was through, she dressed swiftly, almost mechanically, gave me a menacing look as if somehow this were all my fault, and left the apartment. Shahib couldn't look at me and turned to sit at the piano. I ran out after Jennifer, but she was gone. The next day she came to my apartment and brought me a rose. She smiled and left. The following day she returned with an assortment of cookies she said she had baked for me, and we

sat down and ate them together. I could forget things very
quickly.

Jennifer still resides in the trunk of the car in the basement
parking garage. All that remains of her here in the apartment
are the knicks in the harpsichord. It seems to me I have let
this affair dictate my entire existence. In a way I am like those
people who have an expensive funeral and whose lives are
dictated by the arrangements for the deceased. I am bound
to Jennifer simply because she is in my possession. But why
should that be? It's simply a state of mind. My life is ruled
by a corpse. I am no longer free. Let the corpse stay where
it is. I shall ignore it. Now is the time to return to my normal
life. Tomorrow morning I begin a routine day. I shall try to
step back into my familiar life pattern. Nothing will be
altered. Tonight I am very tired. I have done a lot of driving, but to prove my good faith I am now standing before
my magnetic bulletin board preparing for a game of solitaire
ping-pong. My hands are clammy. I am shivering slightly
in a cold apartment. Someday soon the police may even kill
me. But I face the future.

Sixth Day...

Slept late for the first time in a week, waking at 10:00, just in
time for my appointment with Dr. Wasserman. Drove by the
Philadelphia on my way to his office and smiled in at all the people. Most of the kids in my set like to bait their psychiatrists and
I was on the way to prove myself. It's considered very "in" to tell
stories of how you deceived the shrink into thinking you're completely stable when you just slashed your wrists the night
before—or better still for him to write you a prescription for some
tranquilizers or even barbiturates or sleeping pills which you can
alter ever so slightly to make refillable. Jennifer was especially
good at this. She'd play a little girl with the psychiatrist and he'd
want to do anything for her in a paternal sort of way. She'd sit
in the Philadelphia for hours making up stories about these
meetings. She told one doctor she liked to regard his office as a
candy store because she thought all the pills he gave her were such
delicious confections.

Dr. Wasserman's office was on Park in the Eighties. You can tell a psychiatrist's strategy by the kind of art he displays in the waiting room. His had a small Chagall wedding scene, which I suppose was intended to give his patients a subconscious sense of harmony with the world of the family, which hardly any of them ever had. Also it emphasized that this was a Jewish psychiatrist, but this scarcely needed emphasis. I was ushered striaght in and sat down on a leather upholstered chair. The doctor muttered something about couches really making patients feel more ill at ease than relaxed and offered me a cup of tea. It was a standard opening gambit and I was used to it. Relax the patient, be jocularly familiar and assume, in New York, some knowledge or even a large knowledge of psychiatric terminology. Patients are likely to joke familiarly, if in a vaguely deprecating fashion, about "my Oedipus complex" or "my paranoid tendencies." The doctors have become very circumspect, fearful lest their patients outguess them, zig before they can zag. It was just then that I remembered the doctor's name and began to laugh.

"Your name is Sergei, isn't it?"

"Why, yes it is, Marcus."

"What do your friends call you? Do your friends call you Sergei?"

"Some of them do, though not my good friends. My good friends call me Serge."

So far no sign of annoyance on his part. A very cool customer.

"Would you mind if I called you Serge?"

"If you like, though I think you'd feel better if you called me Dr. Wasserman to begin wtih."

Here I had him completely analyzed. He was trying to defend himself and cure me at the same time. He must have assumed my parents were very permissive when I was young—I probably called all their friends by first names. He must place himself immediately in the position of authority figure if he hoped to get through to me. I was baiting him and this was not to be encouraged. Moreover, to protect his own neuroses—and psychiatrists, as we all know, are neurotics—he has to keep that position of power and authority which urged him to his chosen profession in the first place.

"I like Serge better. I called my last psyhchiatrist—Dr. Hyman Frankel—Dr. Frankel, and that never worked. But one could hardly call him Hyman and Hy seemed somehow too jovial to me, like a familiar greeting between American Legion members."

"Then Serge it is. ...Tell me, Marcus, is your girl friend still fermenting in your harpsichord?"

"No, she's now in the trunk of my car."

"Tell me about her. You don't mind if I take notes. You must realize by now that it's a standard technique—and it helps us evaluate the situation better later on. I find notetaking is much less distracting than recording machinery. What was she like?"

His face remained impassive. Get the patient to talk about his fantasies and therewith understand his inner nature.

"It's hard to talk about someone you deeply love."

"It is for all of us, Marcus."

"First of all I think you'd have to call her a Southern belle, although she was never really very pretty, just her long chestnut hair. She was a flirt, though. She'd flirt with all the nuts in New York. She was always looking for approval and the minute she had it, she'd disappear like a shot. One time, when it was storming in June, she rang my doorbell and appeared dripping wet in a secret-agent-style trench coat. 'Do you want to make love?' she asked. I smiled and she smiled back and closed the door and was gone. But it wasn't just that way about love. I suppose most girls have a little of that in them. Even little things like what to order at a restaurant. We'd eat at the best places and she'd order something, look up at me plaintively and ask if that were the right thing. Then when I ordered, she'd berate me as if I had asked for a cheeseburger at the Pavillon. But I suppose the most important thing about her was that she couldn't stand being alone—and the next worse thing to being alone was being in a small group of two, three or four. She loved large groups, and large groups of sickies most of all. That was always a big problem between us. It was why I started having parties, to impress her. I would invite people I'd never heard of before just to make her think I had every important underground contact in New York. Those parties were criminal freak shows, but I can't tell you about them because you'd have me arrested. They were part of the reason I moved out to Jersey."

"I'm a doctor, Marcus. I don't go around having my patients arrested. You'd be surprised how many reports of illegality pass across this desk."

What a pat answer. Anything to encourage my fantasies. If only there were some way to fantasize the truth, but we've carried everything to such unnatural extremes.

"Jennifer and her friends regard abortion as a status symbol. They've been everywhere for abortions—Puerto Rico, Sweden, Japan, Israel, you name it, I wouldn't be surprised if one of Jennifer's friends was the only American in Red China last year for an abortion. Jennifer was impregnated twice by Negroes—I could name names if I wanted to, but the police have now recorded my license plate numbers—and she was aborted both times in Puerto Rico by fancy doctors. I flew with her the second time."

"I think abortions should be legalized, don't you?"

This man was a tough customer, trying to cut the sails out from under me with a quick, quiet remark. He knows I was trying to shock him with exaggerations.

"I don't care about that. I don't care about any of those issues, about abortion, about getting out of Viet Nam, about civil rights. You name it. I'd rather blow pot than stand on a picket line."

"Why don't you do both? A lot of people do."

You may be wondering what I have been doing with my time not recorded in the diary. Lately, I have been sitting in my bedroom with the door barricaded. They may be coming to get me at any moment. I must be ready. My name and address have been recorded by the state police at the toll gate. He probably released me at that time just to taunt me. Maybe the New Jersey National Guard will be mobilized. Perhaps they are in collusion with Ornstein who has been recording my every activity. Perhaps that is why he was so willing to help me dispose of the body. It's like that time in the cave when we were in grammar school, the time I learned to hate him and the time he came always to be part of my life, although I wouldn't see him for years.

"So far every psychiatrist who's tried to help me has been a powerless fake. You all listen with your own ears. You hear what you want to hear."

"We're human beings, too, Marcus, with problems just like yours. What separates the good man from the bad man is his ability to palliate his difficulties so that he can live in society."

"And suppose his way of palliating his difficulties is by murdering or by taking dope?"

"Then we could say that he is a menace to society," said Dr. Wasserman. "Although in certain psychiatric terms he may be completely fit. I would guess it's possible to achieve a sense of harmony and well-being as a murderer or an addict for certain individuals."

"I can assure you of that, Serge."

Dr. Wasserman had risen and was gazing through the blinds at the passers-by on Park Avenue. His office was on the ground floor.

"Is there anything else you can tell me about the dream you had?"

"Dream?"

"Yes, the dream about the girl in the trunk. What's her name?"

"Jennifer, Jennifer Da Silva. She stuttered a lot. That makes her insecure from your point of view. Now all we need to do is discover why she was insecure and she'll be all right. Maybe it has something to do with why she slept around so much. Insecure about sex and love. She took drugs, too. Inner needs not fulfilled. So that's it. Now we know the problem. We can cure her stutter. Only her stutter has already been cured. She's dead in the trunk."

Dr. Wasserman seemed very disturbed and began pacing about. He looked at his watch and I thought he was about to tell me my time was up when he abruptly sat down opposite me, stared with an intensity I had never seen before in broad daylight and said:

"Marcus, would you tell me the truth if it were absolutely necessary for both of us?"

The huge physical presence of Dr. Wasserman began to overwhelm me. I thought, as I had that time in my apartment, of Cesar Romero in distinguished advertisements for high-priced men's clothing.

"Yes, as much as any man can."

"Do you really have a girl's corpse in the trunk of your car?"

I turned momentarily toward the window. A girl was walking by in bell-bottomed trousers, followed by a policeman. I looked back at the doctor as I delivered my answer, conscious that he was looking for its validity in my eyes.

"No. I have very elaborate fantasies."

I am now convinced that he was working with, or at least had complete access to, the records of the state police, particularly those operating near the Tappan Zee Bridge. That Selma awaited me outside of his office corroborated my suspicions. A policeman, I don't know of what division, stood on the corner, but I believe he was a New Jersey state trooper sent across the state line to check on my whereabouts. Selma was all solicitous and took me to the Voisin for lunch for the second time in one week. There's something suspicious in her caring so much about my relationship with this psychiatrist. At the Voisin, I did not make my usual perusal of the dessert table. I came right to the point.

"Selma, what do you know about the southern part of the New York Thruway?"

"Lovely."

"Lovely? That's an awfully vague description from a very subtle directress of a public relations firm, a business concerned with covering up." I betrayed no hint of my motive.

"It's best in autumn when the fall colors dance upon the shores of the Hudson."

"Good. Do you go there often?"

"Not often. Just to see the concerts at Caramoor or when there's a party in the Catskills at the home of some novelist like Saul Bellow. He has a house up there."

"How about driving conditions?"

"Not bad. Planning a trip? Watch out for the state police near there. They're very tough. Heffie and I have had several run-ins with them."

"I suppose you've gotten to know quite a few of the police up around there."

"Well, I'd recognize their faces, if that's what you mean. You get to know them after a while."

"And you call yourself a friend of mine?"

Slowly I rose from the table, unsure exactly where I was going. I headed unsteadily for the men's room. The waiters watched, waiting for me to collapse to the floor. I could not see Selma, but knew that her face would be loathsome to me. The men's room mirror is ornate with gilt rococo edging. I stood looking at my reflection. I wanted to look like a gondolier, but I could not. I was short with a pasty complexion, that suggestion of a harelip. I lifted the syringe from my right pocket with a glassine envelope of heroin. I lit a small fire of paper on the radiator and cooked up the smack in a glass. I was glad there was no attendant in the lavatory during the lunch period. I filled the syringe, found a vein and injected it. It was only the second time in my life I had turned on anything without Jennifer (the other was the peyote with Shahib Lewis almost three years ago), and I felt like I had made a new turn toward freedom in my life. The mirror before me became a portrait from the era of Louis XIV, but then, as had been my habit every time I had taken a narcotic, I thought for a moment that I was my grandfather, moving about, a respected and feared man on the Rialto. I could see all the folly around me. After all, hath not a Jew eyes?

"What's so funny?" Selma asked.

The waiter was looking at us scornfully. And this was Selma's way of telling me to cut out the giggles which had overtaken me since I had left the bathroom. I couldn't stop.

"Would monsieur like a drink?" asked the waiter.

"*Et tu*, Selma," I said, spilling my glass of soda water into my plate. "If I had been given a little sympathy when I was younger, then it would have been different, but no. None of them would bother to look at me. They were all too busy trying to sweep things under the rug. But you, Selma. You were the one I thought . . . you were the only one who would lift me from my cradle, but didn't you realize that the mewling babe in your arms was the dead image of your uncle when he was an infant? My mother always told me so. Selma, you've been a real mother to me, and now you, too. What is a man to think? All around me. The police. We're living in a fascist state. The wires are tapped. People are looking through keyholes. The police use computers to track down cars. Once, if you were rich enough, you'd be safe in the Voisin, but now each cream puff must be checked for strychnine, each napoleon for arsenic."

"Would you like me to take you back to Dr. Wasserman, Marcus?"

"Serge is too busy. Selma, why are you so concerned about me?"

"I'm not concerned about you. I like all my younger cousins."

"You'd still dangle me on your knee if you could—not that I'd let you after I learned you're in collusion with the New Jersey state police. Was it because Old Schlicht could never cut the mustard and give you one of your own?"

"Yes."

Abrupt enough. I lurched forward in my chair, spilling the soda water out of my plate onto one of the Voisin's fancy linens. Selma appeared not to notice. There was a distant look in her eye. She removed her hat and continued to speak in a low rasping voice.

"When you are older, you will realize that we all have our private pains; we are all cripples hobbling through life on a crutch.

63

Sometimes we lean to each other, sometimes we lean apart. As we grow older, we each learn to make our personal adjustments. I have mine. Someday you will have yours."

"You mean Wasserman?"

"Yes. I guess you're old enough to know."

I thought back to the time they came to my apartment and a new evil vision of Wasserman came into my mind, lording it over Schlicht by wearing one of his green berets.

"I want to wear a green beret," I said.

I think my head was rolling in the plate.

"Didn't you get any sleep last night, Marcus dear?"

"Not much sleep. Been out trying to dump Jennifer's corpse."

"You see, dear. Your imaginary girl friend is your crutch as Wasserman is mine. Only Sergei will help you trade in your crutch for one closer to reality."

"But suppose I'm not lying. Suppose there is a corpse in the trunk of my car. Wouldn't I then be a peril to society?"

I blacked out in the Voisin. House passed and the next thing I remember is the electronic twanging of a guitar. Beams of colored light crisscrossed against a wall in front of me. Everybody was dancing. I was dancing, too, with a Eurasian girl with long black hair. She was dressed in a yellow vinyl outfit which ended halfway between her knees and her vagina. Movies were being projected on the ceiling. A color film in blue and red of an Oriental harem, only all the wives were men with their penises dangling out of their saris. The music was provided by three guitars, drums and sax in the city blues style. Raucus.

Ornstein stood there watching as I danced.

"Thank you for taking me among the rich and neurotic, Marcus."

I looked about me. I had been in this place before.

> Born in gangland
> Children of the night
> Got a scar on my temple
> Symbol of what's right
> Yeah, yeah.
> Oh, oh, baby
> Yeah, yeah.

The city blues. Familiar faces all around. Lorraine and Henderson. They were doing the boogaloo. He wore a tuxedo with denim pants.

> *Born in gangland*
> *And I know the score*

My Eurasian friend shook her hair back and forth. Her head tilted back as she communed with the filmic orgy above her. Shahib Lewis danced up and began dancing with her.

"This place is a simulated LSD trip, man. So if you turn on acid here, it's LSD times LSD or LSD squared. Did you make your dump all right?"

Ornstein heard the question and began to shuffle over to the rhythm. Shahib seemed disinterested in the answer and drifted away with Suzie Wong.

> *I'm goin' into the alley*
> *Work over a bum.*
> *I'm goin' into the alley*
> *Work over a bum.*
> *I'm goin' into the alley*
> *Cause that's life in a slum.*

"Makes you hunger for the quiet lakes of New Hampshire, doesn't it?" He was referring to our college days. I wonderd how Ornstein ever found his way to this club. I must really have been out of it to lead him here. This wasn't for peace marchers—although they burned an American flag once—none of these people were ever up in the daytime. Henderson drifted over. His face was made up for the colored light.

"Where's Jennifer? I've got a new dance for her. She's the only one around who's ever for something really new. It's called the 'Lemming.' Everybody freaks out and dances into the wall."

> *Who's got the blues?*
> *Oh, oh well*
> *Mother's got the blues,*
> *Can't you tell?*
> *She's got the blues.*
> *Yeah, yeah, yeah,*
> *She's got the blues.*

I watched Ornstein's face as he talked. It was impassive. I knew he was judging Henderson and I knew his judgments were severe. Henderson was one of those reduced to the state where he couldn't communicate outside of hipsterisms.

"Where's Jennifer?" he continued, pointing upward. "I want to audition for that movie with her."

"You didn't know Jennifer."

"No baby, *you* don't know Jennifer. You don't realize a tenth of the shit that chick's done behind your back. And if you do, your face is covered in it."

Ornstein turned away. I didn't like his pity.

"No, seriously, man, where is Jennifer? This place reminds me of the parties you and Jennifer were running at your old man's."

> *Somethin's got me*
> *And I can't explain it.*
> *Somethin's blowin' me*
> *Out of my mind*
> *A hidden somethin'*
> *That you can't see*
> *Has really got a hold of me.*

"Only this place ain't free."

There had come a point with Jennifer where I always felt I was walking three feet behind her, even when we were arm and arm. A couple of times she even called me "my burden" and we laughed—I desperately, she cruelly. We would meet boys on the street and she would start flirting with them while I stood looking at a shop window. At first I thought she was doing it to hurt me, but then I noticed she never looked at me, never seemed to care how I reacted to her behavior. Finally, one day when we were sitting by the part of Central Park they call Cherry Hill, I suggested we have a party. Her eyes lighted up and she started to dance around the bench doing a hostess act. She would thrust out her hips, offer an imaginary guest some hors d'oeuvres and then when they said yes, she'd look coquettishly down at her sex. That was the afternoon she said to me:

"You know what's denied us rich girls? The need to be prostitutes for money."

We went home and made up a guest list. I thought we should have around twenty friends, but Jennifer couldn't figure out where to end the list, so it went on and on until there were one hundred and ten names. Then we came to the refreshments and I could tell by the look in Jennifer's eyes what she wanted. I thought, for a moment, of those public service messages you hear on the radio: *Don't let others lead you into temptation. Stay away from dope. Sometimes it is more mature to say no.* And all those clichés. but they were only clichés to me even then.

I went to Shahib and asked him if he could think of any surprise for Jennifer at that party. He quietly finished eating the bologna sandwich he had been working on when I rang the bell and said:

"Baby, you're too big for me now. I keep telling you I'm a musician not a connection. I keep supplying you and your nut girl friend from my personal supply. I'm going to take you to meet the Man."

Shahib reached decisively for his coat.

"I've got to warn you as a friend, Marcus. Don't mess with the Man. He's got connections you and I don't know about, maybe with the police, maybe the FBI, Congress, important people in Sicily and Naples, the Cosa Nostra, maybe even the President."

I turned up my collar.

"Don't worry, I learned all about that stuff from my grandfather."

Shahib led me downtown to Larry Dolci's apartment. On the way he explained he didn't really know how high up Dolci was involved in the rackets, only that he was involved in some way. Mafia chieftains rarely live very lavishly. They live humbly so that the style of living gives no clue to their livelihood. Dolci's apartment was primitive. Not like the one he has now. A one and a half room efficiency with flaking walls, barren with the exception of a small crucifix above the head of his bed. Everything was immaculate. It looked as if it had hardly been lived in. The atmosphere of the room was in sharp contrast to Dolci. He reclined on a chaise longue in a cashmere smoking jacket with a cigarette in an elegant holder dangling from his left hand. Shahib disappeared without my seeing him. Dolci asked how I was. What I was doing now. He seemed to know all about me. Knew my family connections. He offered me a glass of Strega, an Italian liqueur, he said, meaning witch. Not a word of my reason for being there. Everything was very elegant, very polite and refined. We might have been two young Italian businessmen sitting on the patio of a villa in Sorrento overlooking the Amalfi Drive. I remarked how young he was to have reached such a pinnacle of success and he said that in his business he had built his reputation dealing with younger customers. It was I who broke the mood of our discussion when I asked:

"Do you ever use your own goods yourself?"

A look of rage swept over his face and disappeared again.

"No, of course not," he replied softly. "Would you like to make a purchase?"

I explained to him what I wanted. He resonded confidently, in the manner of an experienced executive who knows he is representing the better merchandise of a large respected firm. I bought a quarter of a pound of marijuana, the largest sale he must have made in some time, and a small amount of hashish. Then Dolci asked if I wanted any heroin. I told him no, that I didn't use heroin and I didn't think any of my friends did. He asked how I knew. Many people tried heroin these days who you would never expect to. Why not buy some to offer guests at the party? I need not try any myself. It would provide an interesting diversion. I bought two hundred and fifty dollars worth.

Strange to think that the same Larry Dolci was in charge of the section of the Syndicate, call it what you will, which ran the discothèque, The Instant Prince, where I now stood.

"Jennifer's still in the car," Ornstein said. He had me pinned in the corner.

"How do you know?"

"The smell of decaying flesh. I worked for a summer as a hospital orderly."

"It's none of your business."

"Either dump the body or call the police. Indecision is the worst way you can act. You've always been indecisive, Marcus. Always afraid to act, like the time when we were little boys in that cave and you got diarrhea. You stood there, unable to move."

"You don't like to forget things, do you?"

"Get that girl out of the trunk. Act."

"How do you know I haven't been acting in a way you don't know? Maybe I've been acting internally."

I turned away from him to emphasize the drama of my statement.

"I've been keeping a diary of everything that has happened to me since her death. I have recorded all, including my particular motivations. I am a living symbol of the violence of my generation. It will be a masterpiece of criminal pathology."

"Perhaps, if you choose the right events."

"What do you mean if I choose the right events?"

"Well, you can't very well tell every single thing that has happened to you."

"I have revealed the inner workings of the criminal mind."

"Oh. What are those?"

"They are the motives, large and small, that drive a man beyond rational control."

"And what do they tell us?"

I wasn't exactly sure what he meant to imply by that question. There was something familiar about his method of interrogation. It was the method of the state trooper, or rather, the trooper had pre-empted Ornstein's style for that short time I had or had not been guilty of trying to run a toll booth. Further proof of the conspiracy around me.

"I am asking you," he continued, "once we have learned these motives, what do we really know? Does that explain away the act itself? Each act has an existence of its own, above and beyond the picayune, clichéd circumstances which propelled it." He was looking at me straight in the eye. Ornstein never raised his voice when he spoke. Each word was pronounced precisely. I replied:

"Motives can tell us how to...avoid similar problems in the future. We can look at the failings of others...and...and compare them with ourselves." I was stuttering slightly. The music was too loud. "Maybe we can head off problems at the pass...before they...they...reach a...a..."

"A crisis?"

"Yes, a crisis."

"Then your book will prevent us all from becoming Marcus Rottners."

"Yes."

"I hope it is successful."

"Do you think it will be?" I admit this was an embarrassing question. I was placing myself at his mercy.

"I don't know. I haven't read it.

What else could he have said? He couldn't have lied.

"What would you do in my place?" I asked.

"I wouldn't be in your place."

A strobe light was turning us all into strange, ethereal spastics. The fat, Negro drummer sang sitting down with the mike lined up behind the drums.

Mother's got the blues
Can't you tell

Larry Dolci approached from behind the band. He was a serpent-like figure, in a sharkskin suit. He always wore a Homburg hat indoors.

"Another client perhaps," said Dolci, indicating Ornstein while he proffered his silver cigarette case. Our silence was clearly negative.

"Sorry about the little tiff the other day, Marcus, but business precautions must be taken, you read me? How do you like my place? Not bad. We've pre-empted the uptown business. They adore the colored lights. We got the idea for the flickering stuff from the Whiskey a Go Go in L.A. The kids think it's like an LSD trip. Say, Marcus, when are you and the little lady gonna have another party? I might have a special deal on refreshments for you. I could be the caterer eh?" He laughed at his own simple-minded double-entendre, exposing his gold dentures, which made him an even more sinister nineteen. "Well, next time you have another party, you let me know. My friends are very interested in your welfare. Don't let an incident like the other day mislead you. Your grandfather was old Max Rottner. Some important people are still talking about him. Why didn't you tell me? Listen, pal, I've got to take care of business. A new group called Merrill Pierce and the Finches are coming in. They use the fuzz bass and all that psychedelic stuff. See you around, you read me?"

I should have hated him, but I didn't. It was he and his mercenary friends who had first tempted me down the path to hard-line narcotics. If he hadn't sold me those first drugs just for laughs at the party, then that series of events wouldn't have been set off and I wouldn't be a murderer; but then I wouldn't have written this diary, and that is the first substantial accomplishment of my life. I hope it is good, although I wouldn't be surprised if it was terrible. At bottom I have no confidence in myself or in anything I do. But you can't blame a man for anything. If he is evil, he is only a product of his environment; his parents created an evil child. But his parents had parents, and they had parents before them. Can we all place all guilt at the doorstep of some Neanderthalic apes? They didn't even have doors. They had caves. I told all this to Ornstein once and he disagreed. He said we are all personally responsible for our actions, whatever they are. Motives count for nothing. But why am I writing this diary? To explain why I did what I did. To show the world the environment that created my disaster. How can Ornstein be a writer and not believe in the importance of motives? What is there to write about?

Let me show you how a man can be drawn into the web. Jennifer and I sat alone in my New Jersey apartment the eve of that party. Everything had been taken care of. I had made special fifty-dollar gifts to the doormen so that they would be on my side just in case. I had placed tobacco humidors and hookahs around the room. The humidors were filled with generous portions of marijuana. The pipe bowl of each hookah was lined with aluminum foil to prevent it being charred too much by the Cannabis which burns hot. I showed all the preparations to Jennifer and she was duly impressed. Then I led her into the bathroom. The medicine chest mirror reflected the dancing of a sinister Hogarth Rake who hangs above the toilet. On the glass shelf beneath the medicine chest there was a long white cardboard box. I opened it and showed Jennifer the syringe and the glassine packets of heroin.

"So you've gotten up the courage at last," she said.

"You mean you've tried this before?" I asked. I was frightened.

"I've done what I've done. Do I have to report everything I do to you?"

She turned to examine herself in the mirror. She was very sexy in a low-cut black dress which covered only a little more of her than a bikini bathing suit.

"Narcotics addiction is disgusting. You're a slave to something outside yourself. Look at the addict on the street. No future. No help. No self even left. No character except the puny human anxieties built up in search of the next fix. Stay away from it, Jennifer. It's no good for you. We have our own way. The way of the hard-line junkie is different from us. Pot is enough. Do you need anything else to be hip?"

She plucked her eyebrows and applied a thick coat of mascara on her eyelashes.

"Relax, little papa. I didn't ever try heroin, but maybe I'm going to tonight. Don't get worked up about it. But let me ask you one thing. Life is short. Why shouldn't I try heroin if I want to? So what if it kills me. At least I tried something. What have I got to live for anyway? My parents, God, you?"

"Yes, for me. I wouldn't like you to die. I love you, Jennifer."

"You haven't answered my question. Why shouldn't I try heroin?"

I left the bathroom. I didn't know a good reason. The guests began to arrive. First close friends of Jennifer's and mine, then people we didn't know as well. They were dressed as studiedly as possible. Some of the boys wore tuxedo jackets with dungaree or chino pants, or the reverse, motorcycle jackets with elegant slacks, black with a dark silk line down the side of the trouser. I was still living in the apartment facing the Manhattan skyline and the guests began to congregate on the balcony and smoke pot. They all were having a great time being in New Jersey and saying what a unique experience it was.

"The last time I was in New Jersey," said one girl, "was when I was eight years old and my family went to Atlantic City for the Miss America Pageant." Another girl in a leather miniskirt said that although she had been to Hong Kong and Tokyo, this was only her second time in New Jersey; the other time she and a few friends had gone over to Palisades to swim in the World's Largest Salt Water Pool when they were high.

A transvestite who didn't look over fifteen talked to everyone he saw: "Would you believe, New Jersey? Man, this ain't for real."

The girl who visited the Miss America Pageant came up behind him and grabbed his throat. "Do anything to this little lady," she said, "and you break about six kinds of laws. You the host? Nice pad you got here."

"You know, it's remarkable. It only took twenty minutes to get here by bus from Port Authority," said the one in the leather miniskirt, gazing absently toward Grant's Tomb.

Jennifer and I did not talk to each other.

We had agreed not to group together during the party and I knew she didn't want to. Gradually, I began to realize that there were some unfamiliar faces in the crowd. I should have known them, but I couldn't really place them. They looked like my friends, but they weren't. I was worried. The elevator opened directly into the foyer of the apartment. Usually each guest is announced individually from below, but since the party was so crowded, this was impossible. I was about to call down on the house phone and prevent further guests from arriving when I was called over by a group of old friends to tell them the origin of the marijuana in one of the humidors. That was what we liked to discuss: where the weed came from. Mexico, the Texas border, Morocco, the South, somebody's window box (but then the seeds had to come from somewhere). I noticed a conglomeration of people around the bathroom and then a blond, pale-faced girl came walking out with her face in a dull trance. I had forgotten about the heroin. Jennifer must have told them. I tried to place the girl who had staggered out of the bathroom. I looked again, more closely, and realized with a combination of amusement and shock that he was a transvestite. The time had come to halt the flow of unfamiliar faces. I crossed to the house phone, but just then the elevator opened again with a group of about six motorcycle hoods, like the Hell's Angels I met yesterday at the Rip Van Winkle Bridge. Maybe they were the same ones. I couldn't see them at night on the bridge well enough to identify their faces. One of them ran over and embraced Jennifer. I wasn't sure whether he already knew her. "Where's the horse?" another shouted. For a moment I was sure that there were plain-clothes police in the room and that all my precautions had gone to the four winds. The front desk was informed that there were to be no more visitors for the fourteenth floor.

"Why are you closing the party?" Jennifer asked. "Roland de Smoke hasn't arrived, or Muriel or a hundred others I could think of."

"One of these guys could be a hard-line junkie. The police could be on their trail. Follow them right up here in disguise. We'd be finished. My family would be ruined."

Jennifer stared right through me. A group was listening to an old Elvis Presley record, "Heartbreak Hotel," circa 1957, made all the more nostalgic because they were high. Jennifer grabbed the hand of one of the hoods and led him toward the bathroom. Another looked confusedly at a huge bronze statue which faced the elevator door. Jennifer rolled up the sleeve of her hood, kissed his arm just beneath an indistinguishable tattoo, and handed him the syringe. She stood by the doorway and watched while he found a vein and injected himself. I couldn't look. I turned away. I heard a scream. He had pulled Jennifer to him and was frantically tugging at her trying to get her to take the narcotic. I was the only one watching. The others were all in the living room stomping about wildly to the eight-year-old music. Slowly she weakened and he grasped her arm, aimed the syringe and punctured her skin. My head started to whirl as if the heroin were shooting up through my veins. "Help, help," I cried but could barely hear my own voice. I staggered into the other room and began switching the lights on and off.

"Party's over," I said. There was a moan from the crowd. "I have a tip that the police may be here soon."

I could barely speak, but they all heard it. They responded like a flock of sheep to the howl of a wolf. Without pushing they made their way speedily to the elevator. Some even walked down the fourteen floors. Others must have started to run after they were out of sight of their comrades. Jennifer sat in a solemn trance on the toilet seat. Presley was singing "Don't Be Cruel" to an empty room. I tried to talk to Jennifer, but she seemed asleep. I was very depressed. A bad headache was coming on and I could see spots before my eyes. I even contemplated trying the syringe myself as a way of getting closer to her. The thought made me sick to my stomach. I crouched down next to Jennifer and could see that her eyes were beginning to open.

"Let's start all over," I said. "Let's clean ourselves out. We're ugly. We're dirty. There's garbage in our lungs and in our veins. Let's begin again. Again."

I got up and walked over to the telephone, dialed Trans World Airlines and asked if there were any seats on a flight to Venice early that morning. No, but there was space available to Rome and we could easily shuttle on to Venice. I made two reservations on the six A.M. flight to Rome. I told Jennifer as she started to come to. She seemed pleased.

At five A.M. that morning we were at Idlewild and boarded the plane forty-five minutes later. Jennifer had told her aunt we would only be gone for a long weekend, but privately we had decided that if we liked Venice we would stay forever. We slept. At first I enjoyed my dreams, recalling Hagar's offspring and Jacob's staff. Returning to Venice was a true voyage home. It was as if I had been away for a long time, all my life with the exception of that one short visit when Jennifer and I met atop the Hotel Danieli. But then a man came to me in my dream. He said he was Lorenzo and he had come for Jennifer. I told him no, that Jennifer was mine, that I wouldn't let her go. She must live with me forever in our little house in the Ghetto Nuovo near the Rio di Santo Girolamo. But Jennifer came to him and I could see that she loved him. She turned and looked guiltily toward me. Lorenzo clasped her hand and pulled her to him. He was leading her to the Rio Terra Santo Leonardo to the Cannaregio and then down the Grand Canal as he spoke: "Come at once, for the close night doth play the runaway, and we are stayed for at Bassanio's feast."

As the dream Jennifer was fading from my sight, the live Jennifer appeared next to me. I was awakened by the stewardess who brought breakfast. Jennifer remained asleep. I ate and occupied myself with thoughts of escape and release. Jennifer would not wake up, even when the plane landed. I shook her several times, but she would only moan and fall back on the nod. I was becoming very frightened remembering stories of the dangerous toxic qualities of heroin and imagining what would hapen to us if I couldn't pull her through customs. I removed a dexedrine tablet from my toilet kit and shoved it down her throat. For a moment she gagged, but she seemed to swallow it. Most of the passengers were off the plane and the stewardess was coming our way with a courteous smile.

"Is there anything I can do?" she asked.

"No, of course not. We're private citizens."

"Well, I'm afraid you'll have to off-load now, sir. They're going to be taking the plane to a hangar in a minute. If you would like a doctor for the young lady, we would be glad to arrange it."

I slapped Jennifer twice in the face very hard. The stewardess was looking most disturbed and turned up the aisle in search of help, but the other stewardess had disembarked.

"It's people like you who harass this girl, that drive her to this state," I said.

"I'm afraid I don't know what you're talking about. You can take up any problems you have with the Italian authorities at immigration. Now will you kindly off-load or will I have to call the police."

Jennifer was reviving and I lifted her up by the arm, fearful for the moment that I might hurt her where she had been impregnated by the hypodermic. She lurched off the plane and vomited just underneath the left wingtip.

"Air sick," I shouted to the attentive stewardess.

Most tourists arrive in Venice by bus or train. We arrived by train. The railroad station is of a modern design which makes a very unimpressive welcome to a city sung by the poets and painters of antiquity, Lord Byron, Keats, Tintoretto, Canaletto, Turner and, of course, Titian. (These are the names most fequently mentioned in guidebooks to Venice.) The visitor first senses the peculiar quality of this city when he descends the steps of the station and finds no agglomeration of honking taxicabs and frantic pedestrians, but a *vaporetto*, a series of gondolas, and some speedboats. The traveler on a budget will choose the *vaporetto*, a kind of seaborn bus. The luxury voyager will hail his own private speedboat to take him from the Stazione Marittima to his hotel, usually the Danieli or the Gritti Palace. These same voyagers spend at most two or three days in Venice. They must see Milan, or perhaps a scenic trip to Austria is planned. We chose a leisurely ride in a gondola down the Grand Canal. I can be a very nostalgic person, and I thought of the first time Jennifer and I rode the waters and how much younger we were, what a sense of expectancy there was, the beauty of a clean beginning. We glided slowly past the Palazzo Vendramin and the Palazzo Erizzo, past the Ca d'Oro and under the Rialto. Springtime in Venice. I held Jennifer by the hand and we looked at each other misty-eyed. It was like one of these scenes in French movies, when, worldly wise, the two old lovers return together again, this time wary of old mistakes, knowing now that they will be able to control things in the future.

"Honeymooners?" asked the gondolier.

"Just a couple of kids with hot pants," I said.

The gondolier didn't understand. He smiled again, pointing out the romantic Venetian façade.

"For honeymooners, is good place."

"The Palazzo Reale and the Piazza San Marco loomed before us. The Danieli was just ahead. Our gondola pulled up by the hotel landing. The doorman helped Jennifer out of the boat. A porter followed with our two bags.

"Do you have a reservation, sir?" asked the concierge.

"No. We'd like a suite overlooking the Grand Canal."

"I'm afraid we're all booked up, sir. You see, this is the Royal Danieli Excelsior."

He looked at our two small pieces of luggage with a wry expression. Jennifer was still pretty disheveled from the party and I wore my ski parka.

"I wonder if my family suite is available."

"Your family suite?" replied the concierge.

"Yes, the one with the two baths, one in black marble and the other in Carrara white. That's the usual Rottner suite, on the fourth floor, right in the center. My name is Marcus Rottner," I said, passing him my passport, now stamped by the immigration services of twenty-three countries. Jennifer smiled sheepishly and yawned.

"That suite is occupied at the moment, sir. I can give you the one directly below."

"We'll take it," said Jennifer, seeing that I was getting carried away with money-power.

That night we played in the best fashion of the rich. We bathed before dinner, calling sillinesses back and forth from our separate tubs. Mine, the black one, had silver-plated handles; her's, the white, was ornamented in gold.

"Who needs junk when we can have this kind of luxury?" I called out.

The sun was all the way down. A gaily colored gondola sailed by. I could just make out the passengers from my bath.

"Do you think they can see us scrubbing away up here?" shouted Jennifer.

"Cover yourself with a towel. I don't want any lecherous gondolier running up here after you."

"It would be nice to have some pot. I bet it'd be great go-ing for a ride in a gondola turned on," said Jennifer.

"Who needs it? This is great."

Jennifer walked into my bathroom sopping wet.

"Jennifer the Third of Lankershire Castle, Division Da Silva, reporting for duty, sir."

"Sloop the poop, Lady Jennifer."

"Aye, aye, sir."

"When you get through with that, steer the starward-leeward to windward."

"Aye, sir."

"And when you get through with that, report back to me."

"Jennifer the Third of Lankershire Castle, Division Da Silva, reporting back, sir."

"Back so soon, eh?"

"Mission accomplished, sir."

"Good work, Jennifer Three. Climb Aboard."

Jennifer climbed into the tub with me and received a one-gun salute. Then she fell asleep across my chest and slept for almost a full hour. I didn't realize she was awake until I heard her whispering.

"This is a kind of square town, you know?" she said. "I hope the food's good."

"You know the food's good. It was good before."

"Sure is crazy to come all this way to eat dinner in a lousy rooftop restaurant. I've been everywhere in this town. I'm bored."

"That's not the way you felt an hour ago."

"You tricked me into coming with you just because I was high. You were scared of the police. You felt you had to leave the country and you were scared to leave alone."

"That's not so, Jennifer."

"Everything's so quiet here. I'm bored to tears sitting in the tub already. Everything that happened here happened years ago. What do we need it for? I want to go back to New York where the action is."

"Where the violence is, you mean."

"What's wrong with violence?" she asked.

"Nothing, except that it leads to death."

"And what's wrong with death?"

I wasn't sure whether Jennifer was being serious. Her thoughts were macabre, but her voice was gay.

Later we dined at the rooftop restaurant. It had not changed since the time we met and I was feeling nostalgic, tears in eyes and all. Jennifer was eating voraciously, making up for a day's fast imposed by nausea. New York and the party seemed miles away to me, as far figuratively as literally, but I suppose not to her.

"Crying makes you look stupid," she said. "It makes you look like a girl."

"I kind of feel like it's our anniversary."

"Well, what are we going to do on our anniversary? Sit around here and look at all these beautiful things and say my how pretty and get all bleary-eyed? Is that what we're going to do?"

I think that's what she said. Maybe it's only what she says in my memory, but it should be real because it's so distasteful. I wouldn't remember anything distasteful if it weren't real. If I'm not remembering correctly, however, it all becomes a fantasy. But it can't be a fantasy. Dr. Wasserman is wrong. I'll have Ornstein call him and tell him there's a real girl in that trunk.

"What's wrong with a little peace and quiet?" I asked.

"I can't stand it. You talk about death. Peace and quiet is real death. Every time I get in one of those gondolas I think I'm on a boat going across—what's the name of that river?"

"The Styx."

"Yeah, the Styx. So peaceful and quiet, but nothing to do but sink right to the bottom."

"Heroin is more lively, I suppose."

"At least it's an adventure."

"You thought it was some adventure last night. You were frightened out of your mind."

"You were frightened out of your mind. I was sick to my stomach. I would try it again if I had the chance."

"Everybody has the chance. You're a rich girl."

"You're a prude."

"Just because I won't take heroin."

"You're just a general prude."

I had never seen Jennifer eat so much. By now she had finished an antipasto, a large bowl of minestrone, spaghetti with clam sauce, an exotic veal steak done with a peculiar Venetian recipe, which, according to the waiter, dated from the time of the Venetian school of painting (Jennifer wasn't listening) and a fowl dish. She was looking at the menu again. The tears were still in my eyes, but I felt nothing. The accordion sound driftng up from below was incredibly lachrymose.

"You think nothing's happening in Venice. You know who you remind me of?"

"Who?" she asked.

"Lucrezia Borgia."

"That was thousands of years ago."

"It could still be happening now, right out there, without our knowing it."

"The only thing that's happening out there now is some lonely school teacher is falling in love with a gondolier or whatever he was in that movie. It's not that the people around here don't want the modern world. They're just afraid of it."

"And you like the modern world?"

"Sure, I do. Peyote, discothèques, horse, rockets to the moon, color television. That's my world. I'm not afraid of myself."

I was impressed with what she said then, but I was also impressed with the lighted gondolas gliding below me. I didn't know which way to reach and was afraid somehow that if I leaned in either direction, it would slip through my fingers anyway. I'm still not sure I'm remembering what she really said. I don't recall the conversation precisely, or anything that happened in Venice for that matter. I only recall having a memory which began at a certain point perhaps a year ago or less when Jennifer was taking drugs regularly and I was playing along with her. I imagine I wanted to remember a time when things were better, but still these conversations come back to plague me. Jennifer's voice challenging all my simple values. It's not good to kill. It's not good to steal. Excess (drugs, drink) is dangerous. Fidelity is one of the foundations of human relationships. All the things she challenged, or at least she challenged in my imagination, and I had no response. I am not a religious person. I once asked Ornstein about these things and he had all kinds of practical answers. I told them to Jennifer and she laughed and said they did not mean a thing to her. But those communal values, that spirit of love and respect for your fellow man were the things that built Venice, that built the Chioggia and the Palazzo Paladopoli and the Isola di San Giorgio Maggiore and all the canals, big and small, that web the city.

"What are we going to do tomorrow? Can you think of anything interesting?" she asked.

"I can think of a lot of things."

"Like what?"

"We can take a motorboat ride out to the Lido Beach."

"I've been there."

"I know you've been there. But it might be a nice day for the beach. It's a beautiful beach. We can use the paddle boats. It's exciting to swim in a strange sea. Which is it, the Adriatic or the Aegean?"

"How should I know? You're the know-it-all about Venice."

"You don't like to be surrounded by the past?"

"Can't you get it through your thick skull? It's boring. ...I liked the veal steak. That was very delicious. I doubt that you can get one like it in New York." she rubbed her leg against my thigh.

The next morning was a glorious spring day in Venice. The air looked and even smelled clean and the temperature was in the seventies. The people were smiling as they piloted their boats by my window, sailing past with an easy grace more rapid than the previous evening. I expected in the dawning of this beautiful new day, Jennifer would be reborn again, too. She wasn't. She rolled over in bed and called room service for a bottle of Scotch. Then she grabbed some clothes and emerged from her dresing room with her cosmetic bag packed, her sunglasses on and a topcoat draped over her arm.

"After I have a drink, I'm leaving."

"You ordered a whole bottle of Scotch. You might at least stay that long."

"It's for you. I thought you might be lonely after I left."

"I might be. You came all this way, you might as well see something."

"We went through all that last night. There's nothing to see. And I don't feel like going to the beach. I'll just get a sunburn."

"Have you ever been to a ghetto?"

"What do you mean a ghetto?"

"You know, a real Jewish ghetto."

"Oh... sure, the lower East Side."

"They have a real ghetto here. A place where the Jews had to live. They had no choice."

"So what. They do the same things where they have to live and where they live just for the hell of it or because they're afraid to live out with the rest of the world."

A busboy brought up the Scotch and I tipped him. He leered at us and gave me a big wink. I turned the other way. Jennifer opened the bottle and poured herself a shot. She looked at me, but I shook my head. I wanted a glass of orange juice. He had left a copy of the *Rome Daily American* with the whisky. The Warren Commission was under criticism for its single-bullet-theory of assassination. Americans abroad were urged by the State Department to curtail frivolous spending to cut down on the gold flow. Students and professionals stay at the Croce di Malta when in Florence.

"Do you really want me to go with you?"

"What would you do if you were back in New York?" I asked, but of course I knew and I was disgusted.

The walk from the Hotel Danieli to the Ghetto Nuovo is a long one which takes you first away from the Grand Canal and then back in toward it. You leave in the shadows of San Zaccaria Caserma, passing near San Lio and arrive back in the proximity of the Grand Canal near the Teatro Malibran. You walk up the fascinating Via Vittorio Emmanuel in back of the Palazzo Sagredo and the Ca d'Oro. In between the buildings you can see down the *riis* and small walkways to the Grand Canal itself. Once you have passed La Maddalena, you know you are within five minutes of the main square of the Ghetto Nuovo and a few more feet from the Temple Israelitico. I cannot say exactly what happened to me as I drew closer to the neighborhood that day. I had not had any of the Scotch and I was not under the influence of drugs, but as we got to the far end of the Via Vittorio Emmanuel, I became overwhelmed with feelings of anxiety I could not pinpoint. I was no longer annoyed with Jennifer but involved in problems of my own. Jews were passing us in the street, dressed in long dark coats and black hats, sometimes nearly Homburgs like the Jews in New York wear, but more often a tall fez or a cone-shaped hat. They had long hair draping over their ears in the style of pious men. It could have been the lower East Side, but the buildings they passed were older than the United States, as old perhaps as the dream of a land to the West. We came to an outdoor market by the side of the square. I walked up to an old woman selling linens.

"Do you speak English?" I asked. She shook her head and pointed to a man leaning up against the wall reading a newspaper.

"You have pretty girl friend," said the man. "You are lucky. Perhaps you marry."

"Is this all the ghetto around here?" I asked, indicating a broad expanse with my left hand. I felt faint.

"Is no more ghetto in Venezia. Jew may go or come. Some Jew in the United States. Some go to Rome. Some to Israel. Are you Jew?"

"Yes, he's a Jew," said Jennifer.

"But you are not," said the man.

"No, I'm not."

"How come he does not speak Yiddish if he Jew?"

"Maybe he's not a good Jew," said Jennifer.

"He probably brings much pain to his mother and father if he is not good Jew." The man turned to me. "Why you marry this girl if she is not Jewish?"

"We're not married," I said.

"You cause your parents much shame to be with her."

"My parents don't care about that. People don't care about that in the United States. It's a big country. People from all groups come together. They mix."

I was gesturing with my hands and they felt clammy. I clapped them to bring them back to life, but there was no response.

"You look sick. Go back to the United States. Your mother will feed you."

"I live alone."

"If you live alone, you should have wife. Not this wife, but another wife."

"These people are living in the Dark Ages," said Jennifer, waving her arms about. "Look at them. Afraid of the world. Afraid of themselves. Talking in whispers. Selling fruit and linens when there are jet planes flying above them."

I was sitting on a bench between the man with the newspaper and the woman selling linens. I tried to stand, but my knees shook under the slightest pressure. The woman said something in very rapid Yiddish to the man. He turned to Jennifer.

"She says you should take boy home. He might die he look so sick."

I could see down the walkway. Two old men in prayer shawls were entering the Temple Israelitico. I could hear the wailing within as the door swung open momentarily. Then another man walked past us toward the synagogue. The door opened. Again the wailing. The man saw me looking in that direction.

"You want to go?" he asked.

"Oh, no."

"Sure, let's go," said Jennifer.

"You can't go," said the man.

"What do you mean?"

"No women go."

"That's ridiculous," said Jennifer.

"Come with me. We go," he said, his face up against mine.

"No, I can't. We're leaving. This place is too old. Bad memories."

"You come with me. We go. Prayer good for you. You're sick."

"No. We're going back to New York."

"Why don't you go with the old guy? You're afraid of every little adventure that comes along. This is kind of wild. It's like taking a trip in the Dark Ages." Jennifer tried to pull me up to walk to the temple.

"It's no use. I can't move."

"Stop faking, Marcus, and go see the temple with this guy."

"I can't go. My legs won't move," I said, my eyes imploring the man. "Why do I feel such pain? It is my grandfather who was guilty. He is the one who deserves to suffer."

The man was puzzled. "You talk now of your grandfather. Do you have a fever?"

"What judgment shall I dread, doing no wrong? You have among you many a purchased slave which, like your asses and your dogs and mules, you use in abject and slavish parts because you bought them. Shall I say to you, let them be free, marry them to your heirs? Why sweat they under burdens? Let their beds be made as soft as yours, and let their palates be seasoned with such viands? You will answer 'The slaves are ours.' So do I answer you. The pound of flesh which I demand of him is dearly bought. 'Tis mine, and I will have it. If you deny me, fie up your law! There is no force in the decrees of Venice. I stand for judgment.' Answer—shall I have it?"

The old man put his newspaper down and placed his hands on my shoulders. He spoke in a firm voice:

"The quality of mercy is not strained, it droppeth as the gentle rain from heaven upon the place beneath. It is twice blest; it blesseth him that gives and him that takes. 'Tis mightiest in the mightiest. It becomes the throned monarch better than his crown. His scepter shows the force of temporal power, the attribute to God himself, and earthly power doth then show likest God's when mercy seasons justice. Therefore, Jew, though justice be thy plea, consider this, that in the course of justice none of us should see salvation. We do pray for mercy, and that same prayer doth teach us all to render the deeds of mercy. I have spoke thus much to mitigate the justice of thy plea, which if thou follow, this strict court of Venice must needs give sentence 'gainst the merchant there."

> Who's got the blues?
> Oh, oh well
> Mother's got the blues.
> Can't you tell?
> She's got the blues.
> Yeah, yeah, yeah,
> She's got the blues.

The movie of the harem had been replaced by crossing beams of blue and red. Sometimes the beam would sweep so low as to shine in someone's face and then everyone would freeze and the lucky person would dance for all his friends.

The light fell on Ornstein and for a moment I was afraid for him, knowing that he hated being exposed in public and could not dance. He stood there with a wry smile on his face for the duration of the chorus while the light shined on him and all the teeny-boppers and long-haired gorillas thought it was very hip and that he was putting them all on. Suddenly the light swung over to me and all the world was frightening red, like blood streaming in at my eyes. I covered myself from the light and began to scream. I thought it was Jennifer's blood flowing in at me. I yelled "Blood! Blood!" My voice was hoarse and the sound squeaked up through the top of my mouth into my brain.

Soon Ornstein had me by the arm and we were on the street. It was the small hours of the morning and most of the traffic had gone. We walked quietly with only the click of our heels reverberating between the walls of the buildings. We were walking up Third Avenue by musty antique stores. I waited for Ornstein to speak, but he said nothing. The more he waited the greater the weight of his judgment became. Each click of his heel was an indictment of my behavior; yet there was nothing on his face which betrayed the slightest disdain. I knew I couldn't go on living the way I had during the past week. I had to crash through the wall into a new life and it had to be tomorrow. Ornstein must have known this. His footsteps said so. We passed a large antique store that occupied almost a third of a block and Ornstein turned to look inside. A janitor's bulb lighted the store from the rear and I could just make out the flecks of gray in Ornstein's hair. Strange that he should have the vague look of dissipation when it is I who have lived the dissipated life. I still look, as I did when I began this diary, several years younger than my physical age. An old chaise longue was stretched out by the window in front of us, behind that a glass cabinet of the Queen Anne variety. A long row of chairs of various types with legs bowed in and legs bowed out. Some of the upholstery was frayed. Dust covered everything and only a few of the pieces of furniture were protected by a plastic cloth. Ornstein was looking at an object in the rear of the store. He pulled me over and pointed it out to me. It was an old harpsichord, much like mine but in considerably poorer condition, with a plastic cover draped across the keyboard.

"A makeshift coffin," he said. "Note the smell of decaying flesh."

We walked on a few blocks and I followed him as he turned left. We were on Park Avenue and Forty-seventh. Rows of glass loomed before us. It was four A.M. and I could not see another human being for three or four blocks. And then it began to hail, hard stones broke against the pavement and the sides of the buildings. The hail came down hard. We could see fields of it smashing down the side of the Lever Brothers Building. Ornstein buttoned his coat. We stood there transfixed by nature's invasion of modern man's proudest structures. White stones began to collect on the street. They surrounded my shoes. Particles danced before my eyes and landed on my nose. The water of melting ice dripped down from hair and across my forehead.

"I have had enough of this silly charade. Tomorrow is the end. Tomorrow it will be all over," I said. We stood on the patio of the Seagram's Building. The fountains were silent. I looked to Ornstein, but he said nothing.

"Why must you always judge other people?" I asked.

"Why do people always think they're being judged? It's cold out here. Let's walk."

"If you were a publisher, would you want to publish the diary of a young man who killed his girl friend, either accidentally or on purpose, with an overdose of narcotics?"

"If I were looking for something sensationalistic."

"Why can't you give me a straight answer?"

"It's hard to know how to talk to you, Marcus. I never know when you're telling the truth or telling some little prevarication, God knows why, that seems convenient to you at the moment. You're not the kind of person one is honest with."

"I was honest with you once."

"That was under a different circumstance."

"What do you mean?"

"You had to tell the truth. You were in a compromising position."

"You were cruel to me."

"That was sixteen or seventeen years ago, Marcus. We were little boys. I behaved like a child. So did you. No more needs to be said about it."

The hail rattled down even harder between the buildings. The Park Avenue islands were covered with white. So were the streets. The melting ice was beginning to sop through my shoes.

"You see," I told Ornstein, "it is all a very embarrassing memory for me. Some things are easy to repress, especially for me. This isn't."

I felt I was losing control of myself, not in a stupid physical way like when I needed drugs, but deep down, like my gonads were exposed to the elements.

"What can you remember? Can you remember it all?"

"What's all?"

"You can remember I had diarrhea?" I said.

"Of course."

"But can you remember why I had diarrhea?"

"Your parents were getting a divorce. You reacted physically."

"That wasn't what really got me. I knew that was coming for years. But do you remember what I told you?"

"Don't embarrass yourself, Marcus. We needn't go through it. We're men now. We were boys then. I was very cruel."

"You threatened to tell everybody. To make a laughing stock of me in front of the whole club unless...."

"Unless you told me a deep, dark secret. ...Let's cross with the light here."

We were passing a Jaguar sales office. Ornstein stopped to look in the window at a cream-colored XKE. I had almost bought one once, but was afraid it was too ostentatious. I was cold.

"Do you remember what I told you?"

"You mean about your grandfather?" he asked.

"Yes, about him."

"You don't forget those things, Marcus. Stories of gangsters make a big impression on little boys."

"You didn't know he hung out with gangsters."

"No. Not until you told me. You were very upset. A young man with moral scruples."

88

That morning I had begged my mother not to get a divorce. I had followed her around the house, dogging her every step. I threw a tantrum on the living room floor, screaming "No divorce! No divorce!" A big word for an eight-year-old boy. My shoes flew up into the chandelier and knocked a pendant which shattered on an end table. I was sobbing hysterically and rolling across the carpet. Finally I told her she couldn't get a divorce because of what grandfather would have thought. How could she defame the memory of Grandfather Max? For a moment she was taken aback. She ran into the dining room. I followed her, invoking once more the name of my grandfather. I shouted "Papa Max! Papa Max!" at the top of my lungs. My mother was biting her fingers and looking every which way in a frantic search for help. Finally, she grabbed me by the shoulders and lifted me bodily onto the table. She was not a strong woman. "Your grandfather was a hood," she told me. Those were her very words. And then she dragged me into her bedroom and showed me a picture of Max behind bars and another of Max flanked by a pair of hired guns. She told me he was a robber baron who would stop at nothing, a ruthless strongman. I thought my grandfather was a famous man, and therefore great as all famous men were. But she showed me his picture and I knew the truth. There were people like that on television. And besides, I was a very cowardly boy.

"What should I do about Jennifer, Sigmund?"

"I told you a week ago you should report her accidental death to the police. Now you're in trouble. Dump the body."

"Don't worry about being implicated. I won't tell anybody that you helped me."

"I'm not worried. I'd just deny it. It would be my word against yours in court."

"How's the money holding out, Sigmund?"

He didn't answer.

"Did I kill her, Sigmund?"

Ornstein walked off to the right, veering off to the subway station to ride to his uptown apartment. He made a distinct trail among the stones.

"Sigmund," I said, taking his shoulder. "Tomorrow is the end for Jennifer and me, no matter what. I want you to have the diary. Here's a key to my apartment. Go up in a few days

89

and take the diary. It will be under some typing paper in the
bottom right drawer of the desk. Doctor it up. Make it
readable. Do whatever you think is right."

Ornstein took the key. He headed for the subway. In a few
minutes I couldn't see him. Hail. Hail. Hail. Under a distant
street lamp, I could make out the silhouette of a policeman.

Seventh Day...

The seventh day begins here. It should have begun hours ago,
only I haven't slept. I've been writing. Trying to catch up to
date. I know I can't sleep. Too many police. Got to be on my
guard. Got to finish my story. Today is the last day. It has to be.
Can't go on this way. I'm afraid I'll never be able to sleep again.
Can't escape memory. I have no present. Just memories. Just guilt.
And love for Jenny. Oh, Jenny. Keep the police away from me.
Keep the world away from us, like when we came back from
Venice. You loved me then. You didn't need other people. We'd
hide in the apartment for days. Drink until six. Shoot up and hold
hands while it ran through our veins. Love potion, you called it.
I remember when. I remember. Wake up, Jenny. I'm going to go
down to the garage and open the trunk and you're going to be
alive for me. I won't keep you from drugs. I won't be your old
puritan. Not me. Not Old Puritan. Like that time I took you to
meet Larry Dolci and you kissed his cheeks and called him our
milkman I felt so close to you. We were really one. That's love.
Shared experience. You'd get up mornings and go down to the
florist and buy red roses for us to look at when we were high.
Once you bought two dozen carnations and scattered them across
the floor and we'd play pick-up-sticks and you'd say you were
hallucinating and they were hallucinating and they weren't red
anymore, they were orange or green or something. Christ, I wish
I could sleep. I'll never sleep again. Jenny, I'll join you in the trunk.
Get someone to lock us in together. I'll remove the jack and the
spare tire so there'll be plenty of room. We'll be buried together.

I'll leave it in my will. A hundred thousand dollars for a double plot with a white marble syringe over our head, marble from Italy. Only the cops won't know, but there'll be an empty hollow in the middle of the syringe for heroin to drift in over our faces. Dolci would fill it for us. I'd leave him a half a million dollars. And I'd leave money for Ornstein and he could use it to write or give it all to the pacifist freaks or whatever the fuck he wants. Jenny, the police are knocking at the door. I can hear them. Listen, for crissake. They're rattling your trunk. They're coming to get us. They're going to use us for experiments. Make us into freaks. Sap our blood for tests. Sick all the shrinks in the universe on us. Don't let them. Don't say a word. The police, Jenny. The bloody, fucking fuzz. I can see them through the door peep. Thousands of them all in blue. With nightsticks. They're after us. Police brutality. You can't touch me, you shits. I'm a citizen. I've got my rights. Stay away. I've got a lawyer. You can't barge in here without a warrant. They've got machine guns. They've got tanks, bombs, explosives, germ warfare. They're moving in. I'm moving the harpsichord against the door. I'm stacking books on it. All the heavy ones. The encyclopedia. Krafft-Ebing. The complete works of Shakespeare. Dictionaries. The Canaletto. You can't come in here, fuzz shit. You'll destroy a great work of art. I can see his face, Jenny. One of them's got his ugly puss up by the peep. He's looking at me with those fascist eyes. Kill. Kill. Leave us alone. Leave us alone. Now one P.M. Tried to sleep. Could not. Must dispense. Must finish. Must report. Journal comments. Reports all that happens. Act with left hand, record with right. Last chance to explain, to justify. Bleak December. Snow turns to rain. Streets of slush. Stand at window. People sliding. Umbrellas twist. Man falls. Woman laughs. No thunder. No snow. No hail. No sleet. Rain. December. Not even Christmas. Jenny gone. Jenny dead. No sleep. Heroin. Ring elevator. Descend. Garage. Mechanic. Car. Gas. Oil. No smell. Too cold. Frozen, but no snow. Windshield wipers. Defroster. Heater. Radio. Rock and Roll. East River Drive. Brooklyn Bridge. Brooklyn. Police behind. Police in front. Army. Manhattan Bridge. Manhattan. Brooklyn Bridge. Brooklyn. Moving fast. Must escape. Find lot. Jenny.

Memory:

Sometimes
when happy. We eat
leave food
under pla
te just to t
rick bourg
eoisie
We happy to
hats

love. We happy. Never
again. Gondolier. Padd
le boat. To safety. H
ow to explain? Hate se
lf, love Jennifer. Gondo
lier. What matter she
bitch? She safe. I lov

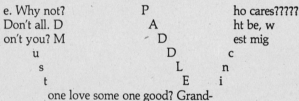

e. Why not?   P   ho cares?????
Don't all. D   A   ht be, w
on't you? M   D   est mig
    u   D   c
    s   L   n
    t   E   i

one love some one good? Grandfather. Jennifer

Brooklyn again. Empty lot. Junk. Refrigerator. Car seat. No
sounds. Gulls. Garbage. Rain. Open trunk. No, won't look. Close
trunk. Leave here. Must dispense. Open trunk. Close trunk. Open
trunk. Close trunk. Open trunk. Close trunk. Open trunk. Close
trunk. Sex. Open trunk. Jenny. Pants. Button. Pull. Sex. Do.
Dead. Love. Do. Sex. Sad. Lonely. Ouch. No. Done. Pants.
Close. Lid. Trunk. Rain.

Memory:

S
h
e

s
a
i
d am falli
ng help me
inject dou
ble dose s
he said in
ject more,
more, more
she said, I
repeat she
said she
was fallin
g asleep m
ore bomb t
a hit it h
ard each m
an decides
for himsel
f she asks
she gets b
ut it was I who pushed the
p
l
u
n
ger

Drive. Brooklyn. Queens, Nassau, Suffolk, no matter. Jamaica,
Forest Hills, Bensonhurst, Garden City, points west, points south,
points east, ocean, gulls and away. Just drive. More gas. Drive
and drive. No junk. Yes junk. Yes junk. Bathroom. Needle. Grace.
Car. Drive. Hours. Vision. Windshield. Nausea. East Hampton.
Windmills. Winter. No one. Ornstein. Seventh day. Must have.

To send. Mailbox. Must complete. Too late? No hope. Seven days. Good number. People think. Why? Cause it took, seven days. Seventh Day Adventist. State police. Town police. County police. Army. Militia. Minutemen. Functionaries. Officials. Night watchmen. Guards. Pinkertons. Bus drivers. Ticket sellers. Police. Uniforms. Police. Police. To escape. Where? Island. No police. No uniforms. No rules. No parents. No. No. Island. Canals. *Riis.* Hills. Adirondacks. Appalachians. Rockies. Pyrenees. Alps. Urals. Himalayas. Helicopters. Rescue teams. No. Crowds. Masses. Throngs. New York. Cairo. Hong Kong. Calcutta. Poverty. Starvation. Pickpockets. Perverts. Strikes. Famines. Uprisings. Tear gas. Riot squads. Mass murder. Gestapo. No. Immolation. Death. Maybe.

Must return. See Dolci. Ask what to do. Syndicate. He knows. Cosa Nostra. Mafia. Black Hand. Money. Buy help. Dispense body. Satellite. Submarine in Pacific. Grave in Sicily. Some way. Suffolk. Nassau. Queens. Brooklyn. Williamsburg Bridge. Manhattan. Houston Street. East Side. Dolci. Ring bell. No answer. Park car. Wait. Police. Gone. Wait. Wait.

Gondolier. Hypodermic. Jewish star: Memory.

Dolci gone to Jersey. Mafia hideout in Newark. Home to Jersey and fumes. Follow him. Through Lincoln Tunnel. Home to Mother Jersey. Air and dirt. Like a magic genie come the fumes of Jersey. Sulphur plant. Vacant lot. Try Mafia warehouse. Try Dolci and Magia. Sit and wait. Try Dolci again, sit and wait, sit and read the *Daily News,* mind fogs in slowly as the rain turns to sleet which oozes down the windshield and sit and sit in Jersey near Newark and wait as the cops walk by and the people walk by and the people and the cops and the cops and the people and read the *Daily News* read Wanda Hale and Bob Sylvester and the Inquiring Photographer and the Voice of the People and read the editorials and read the news and try Dolci again and again and hours pass and people pass the cops pass and wait and cops pass and look and read the *News* the sports and the ads for the nightclubs and go-go joints and the neighborhood movies and try to sleep a little but can't just numb not able to move watch the cops pass with the people watch the cops look at me one or two of them trying to decide who I am sitting here and sitting here and sitting here and trying the door of the warehouse across the street but no answer maybe he's on Palermo or some other Mafia place in New Jersey or the mountains where they all hang out maybe

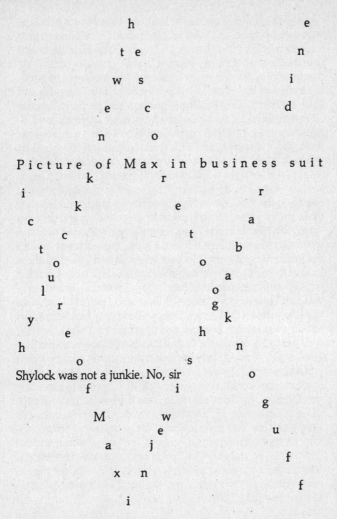

Picture of Max in business suit

Shylock was not a junkie. No, sir

the cops should be there looking after them and not worry about
me three girls pass and look at me and are about to smile but don't
they must think I am ugly but all I am is tired so tired and unable
to sleep just waiting and waiting for Dolci to come to make a sale
to make contact my only chance the weather being what it is the

sleet and the *Daily News* maybe I can buy tomorrow's *News* the cops pass by again and look and look closer I wait and scratch my neck and scratch my back and read Wanda Hale again and read all the columns again because I usually miss something the first time through as the cops cross back and look right in across the front windshield and they are washed out by the slush and sleet and that junk as I shift my position and prop my head up on my arm and then a cop wraps a few times against my wind-shield and then I think he's gone away and a few minutes later or maybe longer he comes back with a friend and they stroll by and look in and then come back and knock on the door and I start reading the *News* as if I didn't hear them and they wrap again and they knock again and I look up and they motion for me to roll down the window and I pretend not to understand but they make things very clear so I roll down my window and they ask for my identification and I look for my identification all over and it isn't anywhere and it's not in the glove compartment and it's not under the seat only I do have a license and I have all those kind of things like license and registration and finally I find my wallet in my back pocket where my wallet usually is and I take it out and two empty glassines fall out and I put my foot down to cover them and the Jersey trooper moves my foot with all his strong weight which is so much stronger than my weak foot and they put handcuffs on me and all the time I am writing and they are looking at me queerly because I am writing and they can't understand and I am wondering why they don't stop me but they don't maybe because they're afraid of writing cops like that and they begin to search the car while I lean against the trunk and the other cop takes the keys and starts to open the trunk but I lean harder and harder and sprawl over the back and my shirt is sop-ping and they're wearing slickers and I've just got a shirt and one cop pushes me away and the trunk flies open and Jen is there and they look at me and they have eyes of triumph like they've discovered gold or invented how to live forever and they don't know how much I love. ...

S. O.'s Account

On that day, June 13, 1967, it is already hot in the northeast section of the country. This includes Newark, New Jersey, where three old ladies and a young Puerto Rican sit on a bench opposite the courthouse fanning themselves. A maximum of ninety-three is predicted by the *Times*. The news is unsettling as a war-torn world moves into another difficult summer. George Tomeh, Syrian Ambassador to the United Nations, had just accused the Israelis of breaking the ceasefire agreement of the Security Council and moving their troops to more advantageous positions, ostensibly to strengthen their hold on water supplies. The Israelis have issued a firm denial. The middle of the paper is filled with discussions of the rapid Jewish success in the Middle East War and reports of inner dissension within the Arab states. On the home front, "Black Power" advocate Stokely Carmichael has been jailed on successive nights as Negro rioting has broken out again in Alabama and Georgia. Quaker groups offer a solution to the Viet Nam problem and a professor at a small college in Pennsylvania has lost tenure because he staged a "study-in" on Southeast Asia during campus Leadership Day. Certain students picket urging his reinstatement. Lafayette Radio is staging a three-day sale. Lafayette LR 300 AM FM Stereo Receiver, Garrard Model 50 Turntable, Pickering V15/AT2 Diamond Stylus cartridge, two Lafayetter Dekorette V-slim speakers for $189.95. A seven-piece guitar for $16.95 and a deluxe 4-way Car Emergency Flasher $3.88. The Bugaku, Japanese Puppet Theatre, offers their last six performances at the City Center. Not much new in sports. Muhammed Ali is facing some difficulty with his draft board, but hopes to fight in Sweden anyway. Murphy Racket paid $12.80 at the fifth race at Yonkers. NEVEL—Alex R., on June 12, of Benoza, Pa. Funeral service at the Jennings Memorial Church of St. George, Lister Ave. and Whisby St., Ardmore,

Pa., on Wed., June 14, at 2 P.M. Interment private. Also, although unlisted in the paper, Marcus Rottner, herewith called M. R., appears before Judge Arthur McGuane of the Supreme Court of the State of New Jersey for the plea on his case Docket #4114. He has been arraigned by a Grand Jury in Newark and since the crime was peculiar, they had some difficulty settling on the nature of the indictment.

The New Jersey Statutes Annotated, Title 2A, Administration of Civic and Criminal Justice offers some help to the lay reader. First, was a murder actually committed?

2A:113 Murder

If any person, in committing or attempting to commit arson, burglary, kidnapping, rape, robbery, sodomy or any unlawful act against the peace of this state, of which the probable consequences may be bloodshed, kills another, or if the death of anyone ensues from the committing or attempting to commit any such crime or act;... then such person so killing is guilty of murder.

There are, of course, first and second degree murders. For example, in New Jersey, when a defendant subsequently withdraws from a suicide pact, that is considered first degree murder *(State* vs. *Collins)*. If, however, the accused's mind, because of worry, drugs, disease, or want of rest, was prostrated to an extent making him incapable of specific intent to kill, the offense is murder in the second degree, *(State* vs. *Close)*. Whether M. R. committed murder is significant because murder, in New Jersey, is most frequently punishable by death. The area of "intent" and the related question of "premeditation and deliberation" are crucial. To an existentialist an act itself constitutes premeditation. To do, in a sense, is to have planned. All deaths are murders. The State of New Jersey, nor any other state for that matter, does not agree with this view, but in *State* vs. *Pierce*, the court decided that the time of premeditation may be very short indeed—time enough only to lift an ax or, for that matter, to point a syringe. Defense was hoping for a charge of manslaughter.

2A:113-5. Manslaughter

Any person who commits the crime of manslaughter shall be punishable by a fine of not more than $1,000, or by imprisonment for not more than ten years, or both.

Had Defense known of the existence of the diary it might have found it useful in the preparation of the case, because most likely it would have been admissible in a New Jersey court. Previous rulings listed under "conduct of accused after killing, evidence of" such rulings as *State* vs. *Barth, State* vs. *Neary* and *State* vs. *Schuck* supported a lenient New Jersey attitude toward admissibility. The defendant was indicted for first degree manslaughter, particularly under the "negligence" statutes. He was also indicted under various narcotics statutes and other New Jersey rulings concerning the failure to report a dead body to the county coroner's office.

Although announcement of the plea was not noted in the *Times* of that day, M. R.'s adventures were documented to some small extent in the press. Coming, as they did, amidst the growing tensions of the Middle East, they were forced well off the front page, but the garishness of his crime and the wealth of his background necessitated at least a follow-up article in the more sensationalistic press. The only daily to run a picture was a Newark paper that used a college graduation photo of Mr. R. One of the weeklies which cater to the pornographic trade published a photograph of a harpsichord with the caption: "Teen Junk Girl Lodged Within." The harpsichord was not M. R.'s. Even this particular scandal sheet grew weary of the incident. After all, since Richard Speck, Charles Whitman and the gunning down of James Meredith, a story such as this one has become a little puerile. The young literati, some of whom knew M. R., are still somewhat interested. What is his significance? Did you know him? Have you heard of him? Vicious rumors spring up. They are forgotten.

Drugs among the middle class are already an accepted national phenomena. If not heroin, at least LSD. Important men pronounce on the situation. George H. Gaffney, Deputy Commissioner of Narcotics, says students take drugs "because of the growing disrespect for authority, because some professors don't care to set any kind of moral influence and because of the growing beatnik influence."

Dr. John D. Walmer, director of the mental health clinic at Penn State, believes "for people who are chronically unhappy drugs bring some relief from a world without purpose."

Dr. Harvey Poweson, director of the psychiatric clinic at Berkeley, sees users as dropouts from the Great Society.

One father woke his son late at night with a long distance phone call from Bangkok. He had learned of M. R.'s arrest on a teletype. He told his son to say nothing if the police asked any questions and to direct any problems to his lawyer. The son, then a graduate student at one of our prominent universities, had not as yet heard of the scandal. The news broke earlier in the Orient. Death by heroin crossed the international date line.

The hot dog vendors opposite the Newark Court House realize a case of some minor significance is going on. A few more than the usual number of "trial buzzards" have forgone their second dog with mustard and hot onions to hurry in. The trial attracts a small crowd of drifters and hangers-on and rich, upper-class Bohemians who either know the defendant or his name. Some interested in neurotic manifestations of our time attend. Men appear in conservative Brooks Brothers suits and in new English-style, double-breasted combinations made of an elegant wide-wale corduroy bought either abroad or at an artsy men's store like the Casual-Aire. Two teeny-boppers enter arm in arm with their beaux. They wear miniskirts and their hair hanging straight down with the bangs cut low over the eyes. The boys wear floral pattern shirts and tiny "poor boy" hats perched on top of their heads. The court reporters look around to see if any of these kids are "turned on," if that's what they call it. It would make good copy if the police would stage an arrest right here in the Supreme Court of the State of New Jersey. Maybe one or two of the Syndicate people will be implicated. Larry Dolci is not here, however, and he's rumored to be spending a few weeks in Puerto Rico. Shahib Lewis is nowhere to be seen. Order in the court. A man stands up and leaves. His wife is in tears. Someone whispers she may be a relative. All rise for the judge. The judge enters. A teeny-bopper calls to a friend who is on the other side of the benches. The friend tries to cross over but is blocked by a policeman. The clerk calls the defendant. The friend shrugs her shoulders and turns to watch carefully as the defendant is brought in. Two young novelists are taking careful notes, giving a full description of M. R. as he first appears. Is he nervous? How is he dressed? Will he talk back to the court? Does he look at anybody, give any nods of recognition? All negative, very banal, very disappointing. Everything too underplayed, like a bad documentary. The young novelist to the left looks pensively toward the ceiling, then lifts his pencil again. Perhaps he is not a novelist at all. Perhaps he is a playwright. The court calls counsel and then the defendant to the bench. Some of the young men in the front rows lean forward to hear what is going on. The "trial buzzards" do not disturb themselves. They know it is impossible to hear. Counsel then announces the defendant's decision to change his plea to guilty on all eight counts. Some discussion goes on of little or no interest, simply reiterating the material of the indictment. The date of sentence is settled for a month hence. Case dismissed. A couple of acquaintances nod to M. R. Others go off bewildered, wondering why nothing very exciting happened. For some it is their first trial away from the extenuating circumstances of a television series or a who-done-it. M. R.'s expression has not changed the whole time. He is impassive, with the stubbornly unemotional expression of a child who is trying to be more grown-up than his parent by showing no reaction to a difficult situation. Underneath he derives his strength from his inner superiority. Also, he wears no tie, a last-ditch attempt to flaunt convention in the most mundane manner. Outside the courthouse, one of the young novelists is taking some last notes before taking his leave.

The question of how to punish M. R. is a puzzling one. Obviously he is not entirely guilty because he does not have complete control of himself. The psychiatric terms are useless by way of definition. Psychiatrists did not seem to have much success with him anyway. He is simply a sick young man in a sick society, a kind of a small, impedimentary cancerous growth on outmoded, imperialist tissue. You operate on the growth and excise it, but the operation will only be a success if the cancer was benign. The other alternative is to raise the society at its roots. "Torpedo the Ark!" Ibsen said. In *Réflexions sur la Question Juive*, Sartre finds that the only answer to anti-Semitism is to abolish bourgeois society as we know it. As long as there is a middle class, the need for prejudice and the invention of scapegoat groups will exist. The state and the family themselves were developed, according to Marx, to hold the classes in check. The signs of violence in America today—M. R., the Viet Nam war, the multiple murders, racial violence, automobile deaths, slum poverty—are only signs of a capitalist society in decay. But we've known that for years. What a towering irrelevancy. Let them skewer M. R. in the President's barbecue pit. Let them throw him to the lions or to the Christians. What difference does it make. What possible effect can it have in a country where Jack Ruby is just an average Joe and Lee Harvey Oswald is simply a young man who saw the light but was too stupid to know what to do with it.

No one can know the validity of M. R.'s journal, although it can here be attested that the scenes with a certain S. O. are fairly accurate. M. R. was always generous with S. O., if only because he was embarrassed in front of him, embarrassed because S. O. was always and is always *engagé* in the French style. M. R., it appears however, was never really aware of the true nature of S. O., but he saw the externals and the externals are finally more important. We can spend so much time analyzing motives and then history will pass us by. Suffice it to say that some members of this society are M. R.'s and some are S. O.'s but they are both aberrations, both cancers in the inexorable mainstream. If the Ark was torpedoed, they would go down with the masses. Even Ibsen himself would sink.

It must be admitted that S. O. thinks the journal is in some ways pathetic. It is pathetic how M. R. attempts to put some of the blame for his activity on a certain Portuguese girl, J. D. S. So J. D. S led him into this. J. D. S. led him into that. We are lucky he did not have the courage to blame everything on his parents. We were spared long discussions of the agonies of a child in a broken home. Instead there are the pseudo-mystical allusions to grandfather identification. Here we may see the true workings of American history. His grandfather is a product of the era known, not popularly but only to

S. O., as "Jewish Power." During those early days of this century the Jews sought to step into the bourgeois structure of American society. They would move into finance, education and the professions. They were thwarted, but they eventually moved in. Today they are secretly hated and their children have turned aberrant, like M. R. In like manner, if the Negroes are lucky enough, they will be able to move up the power structure from poor junkies to rich junkies.

S. O. avows that he is not a joiner. He carries no cards. He swears no allegiances. But the times are such that he finds himself against the wall. The forces of evil are pushing him off the island. One must act to show where one stands. *C'est l'heure.* Leif Ericsson must have known something when he found America and decided not to stay. In the interim between M. R.'s plea and his sentence, S. O. has joined a small group of anarchists forming along eighteenth-century anarchist lines. At first he is reluctant to identify with the group. They are too extreme. At heart he is as conservative politically as he is socially. They frequent bars on the Upper West Side and discuss affairs of the day. One of them is an expert in computers who soon plans to take apart strategic government cybernetic installations. Another is a poet who no longer writes and now reads books on arson. A third spends much of his time in Dallas trying to link the CIA with the assassination. Often they ask S. O. about the character of M. R. The word is about New York that S. O. knows the inside story of the youthful addict. People stop him on the streets and ask what really happened. Are the cops telling the whole story? S. O. objects because all this socializing cuts down on his writing time. Other times he must do certain missions for this group. They have discovered he is a writer and are prevailing on him to write small propaganda leaflets to be distributed among students and intellectuals and some special broadsides to be posted in key areas should a disaster take place on a national level which would be to their advantage. Some of these disasters they themselves talk about, but thus far none has acted. They are cruel, brazen acts to no specific political purpose. The members of the group realize this, but hesitate to choose a political ideology or vantage point from which to attack society. All establishments are suspect. One day the Americans offer something and the

Russians refuse. The following day the Russians make the same offer and the Americans refuse. America refuses to allow Red China admission in the United Nations. Red China refuses to join the United Nations if admitted. S. O. writes political parodies using these paradoxes of international power as his major motifs. He and the members of his group have taken oaths of extreme asceticism. They do not smoke. They do not drink. They make love in yoga positions and exercise daily. They toyed with the idea of allying themselves with other interest groups, with the Fruit of Islam to provide for their defense, but have decided that this is not the time for coalitions. Even the Provos of Holland seem too ambitiously optimistic. There is no direct answer to the problems of human behavior. All positive programs are insane. The time has come for this small, select group to quietly go about dismantling the bombs on both sides, especially since the principal parties have no intention of doing it themselves. The famous blackout of New York City in the fall of 1965 may have been their first work. They may now be working on a plan to blackout the entire world's power supply, the genius of international technological anarchy.

There were no funeral proceedings for J. D. S. She was buried very quietly about two days after her discovery in the trunk in a quiet, out-of-the-way cemetery in Southampton, New York, near her aunt and uncle's home. They were at once shocked and relieved. Her mother came to watch the burial with a curiously blank expression on her face, but her father, after immediately sending a telegram expressing profound alarm, followed this a day later with a cable saying he would be unable to come for business reasons, dated Trieste. Unlike M. R., the minute J. D. S. was entombed underground, she was forgotten. Her family was not the scion of a public relations empire and besides the youth was still alive, somewhat the center of attention.

The month of June passed into July, but the weather did not change visibly. The summer of 1967 was wet and sticky. Whatever joy people found in life, they did not find in the world around them, but in themselves. The first week in July saw six days of unremitting rain. A member of S. O.'s group reflected that the flood had returned. And then there was one nice early summer day, and then the rains returned again.

It rained and rained, only subsiding, as if by divine intervention, at night, until the day before M. R.'s sentence. It was cool and clear that night, and the parks were filled with people perhaps overanxious to greet the arrival of the sun. The following day, the day of the trial itself, the temperature stood at seventy-eight. Couples walked arm-in-arm though Central Park and Borough Park and Washington Square and Foley Square, in fact through all the parks and squares. Some of those close to us were not lovers that day. Larry Dolci, sporting a handsome Cape Cod suntan, sat very near the front of the courtroom, as if taunting the judge with the image of international crime itself. Seated closer to the rear was that sometime lover Dr. Sergei Wasserman. His paramour Mrs. "Heffie" (Selma) Schlicht sat on the other side of the room, careful to look only once or twice in the direction of her good friend, the graduate of the New York School of Psychoanalysis. One or two other members of the family were there, but, although their roles may be important from a deterministic point of view, that point of view is itself unimportant and we shall let them write their own diaries. S. O. was there, of course, thinking the words with introduce Baudelaire's *Les Fleurs de Mal*: *"Vous, mon semblable, mon frére. ..."* Although S. O. may have carried some kind of bomb, a Molotov cocktail or a plastique, in his pockets, his mind was filled with literary allusions. He thought of society's fascination with the demented and how they act out our secret wishes for us. Years ago, this was different. We all wanted to be romantic nihilists, like Pechorin in *A Hero of Our Time*. But now, with all the violence, we dream of ourselves dragging the carcass of our lover through a deserted street in a once thronging metropolis. All is dead, even ourselves—and we do not bemoan our death. We laud it.

All stand for the judge. All sit. M. R. looks tired. He seems to want to go to sleep. For a second he closes his eyes and his attorney nudges him. S. O. asks himself again what punishment he would give M. R. Sergei Wasserman asks himself the same thing. One relative hopes he will be put away a long time until he is forgotten. But he will be forgotten soon in the welter of disaster which shall overtake his own country. A lot of technicalities are discussed, but people seem to have lost interest since the last trial. The teeny-boppers are no longer with us. The older people are more self-conscious because they are more visible. They feel somehow the condemnation of the press. You are guilty. You are the ones who made this young man this way. But, Mr. Gentleman of the Press, sir, we have other children who are upstanding citizens. Why one of them—no, that's no use. The defense attorney is about to speak.

"Your honor, please, I realize this is a complicated case fraught with overtones, nay, overburdened with them, complexities of our day with ramifications, both sociological and psychological, beyond the scope of what is readily our concern with current purview vis-à-vis the legal process. Your Honor sees before you a young man who has found himself a victim of vicious forces entrapping the youth of America today and he is, after all, a first offender."

An interruption by the District Attorney's office as both counsels discuss something at the desk. The Defense resumes.

"The psychiatric briefs filed with you in the usual fashion, Your Honor, state that certain redemptive measures may be envisioned by correctly trained personnel. And this we recommend. I need not remind Your Honor that this young man is by some mark far exceeding the common mean of intelligence, and could take an important, perhaps even a leadership role in our society as we know it."

There is something insecure in the lawyer's voice and M. R., for the first time in two days of trial, lets out an audible groan of disapproval. Both Defense and the District Attorney turn toward him with a look of annoyance.

"Your Honor, psychiatrists agree that this young man wants most of all to live a life free from narcotics and their pernicious ensuant evils."

M. R. turns away with a frightening grin on his face. All are afraid he will break out into laughter or into hysterics. The family is somewhat apprehensive. They have hired a New Jersey lawyer against their better wishes. Also they allow no New York counsel to sit with the defendant for fear of antagonizing the Newark authorities.

The defense attorney has completed his drone and the District Attorney is shuffling about restlessly preparing to speak. Just then, the first group of teeny-boppers enters and all turn around to watch them find a place. One of M. R.'s relatives tries desperately to disassociate herself from these children by the resigned look on her face. Selma Schlicht does not wear her red hat. The Court recognizes the District Attorney. He is already *in medias res.*

"While we agree, Your Honor, with distinguished counsel that the defendant was a victim of certain circumstances, shall I say vicious circumstances, surrounding the youth of today, the Court would not be well served by leniency. We need only look around us to see that we are setting an example for others who may find the path of the defendant attractive, even romantic."

M. R. looks at S. O. Their eyes meet. Nothing is related. They have nothing to say. They have nothing in common. S. O., for all he might try, would never be an enemy of society; M. R. is a born parasite, clinging to the world by an umbilical cord now beginning to fester with communicative diseases. He turns from S. O. with a hint of disdain. Something deep in the retina of his eye is enjoying the triumph of degradation, the knowledge that one has seen the other side and must ascend now, and ascend with a surety of footing that those others of us, like S. O., will never have without subjecting ourselves to public ridicule.

The judge moves to pass his sentence, but a sudden boredom comes over the entire room. It is as if nobody any longer cares. The spectacle is over. The defendant himself is scarcely listening. The Court and all its constituents are bored. The trial stops in time. The judge raises his hands and moves his mouth and passes sentence, but nobody realizes what it is. Nobody could hear, even if they wanted to. The defendant makes his closing statement in silence. The press is reminded that the trial is over. All file out into the air, though none speak to each other. Days pass before the trial really takes place and the actions catch up with the realities; and when they do, we realize why we were so bored in the first place.

J. D. S. remains dead, although there are some of certain persuasions who believe she has risen or perhaps has even been relegated to an excruciating eternity.

S. O. has gone to Canada with his group. He still has a small amount of M. R.'s money. There they hope to avoid participating in a war whose name they can scarcely remember. Their only fear, and it is this fear that keeps them alive, is that they will be extradited and made to return to their native land to fight in that war whose name they have forgotten. When last heard of, they were moving north into the Yukon Territory, bombing bridges as the went. The Royal Canadian Mounted Police have no precise record of their whereabouts.

M. R., of course, resides in jail. He does not do much of anything. He sits, but does not think. Once every two days, he meets a psychiatrist who tells him that if he can learn to come to terms with his past he will be able to take his place as a responsible member of society. M. R. does not think about this when he sits alone in his cell. He jail term is of moderate length, but even that does not impress him. Perhaps he will make something out of himself, build his mind in the jail library. Maybe his creative powers will flower in prison like the Marquis de Sade's. Maybe not. In either case it is very boring.

Thus ends the story of our three friends, S. O., J. D. S. and M. R. Our task was only to entertain. A great while ago the world began, with hey, ho, the wind and the rain, but that's all one, our play is done, for the rain it raineth every day.

BLACK LIZARD BOOKS

JIM THOMPSON
AFTER DARK, MY SWEET $3.95
THE ALCOHOLICS $3.95
THE CRIMINAL $3.95
CROPPER'S CABIN $3.95
THE GETAWAY $3.95
THE GRIFTERS $3.95
A HELL OF A WOMAN $3.95
NOTHING MORE THAN MURDER $3.95
POP. 1280 $3.95
RECOIL $3.95
SAVAGE NIGHT $3.95
A SWELL LOOKING BABE $3.95
WILD TOWN $3.95

HARRY WHITTINGTON
THE DEVIL WEARS WINGS $3.95
FIRES THAT DESTROY $4.95
FORGIVE ME, KILLER $3.95
A MOMENT TO PREY $4.95
A TICKET TO HELL $3.95
WEB OF MURDER $3.95

CHARLES WILLEFORD
THE BURNT ORANGE HERESY $3.95
COCKFIGHTER $3.95
PICK-UP $3.95

ROBERT EDMOND ALTER
CARNY KILL $3.95
SWAMP SISTER $3.95

W.L. HEATH
ILL WIND $3.95
VIOLENT SATURDAY $3.95

PAUL CAIN
FAST ONE $3.95
SEVEN SLAYERS $3.95

FREDRIC BROWN
HIS NAME WAS DEATH $3.95
THE FAR CRY $3.95

DAVID GOODIS
BLACK FRIDAY $3.95
CASSIDY'S GIRL $3.95
NIGHTFALL $3.95
SHOOT THE PIANO PLAYER $3.95
STREET OF NO RETURN $3.95

HELEN NIELSEN
DETOUR $4.95
SING ME A MURDER $4.95

DAN J. MARLOWE
*THE NAME OF THE GAME
IS DEATH* $4.95
NEVER LIVE TWICE $4.95
STRONGARM $4.95
VENGEANCE MAN $4.95

MURRAY SINCLAIR
ONLY IN L.A. $4.95
TOUGH LUCK L.A. $4.95

JAMES M. CAIN
SINFUL WOMAN $4.95
JEALOUS WOMAN $4.95
THE ROOT OF HIS EVIL $4.95

PETER RABE
KILL THE BOSS GOODBYE $4.95
DIG MY GRAVE DEEP $4.95
THE OUT IS DEATH $4.95

HARDCOVER ORIGINALS:
LETHAL INJECTION by JIM NISBET $15.95
GOODBYE L.A. by MURRAY SINCLAIR $15.95

AND OTHERS...
FRANCIS CARCO • *PERVERSITY* $3.95
BARRY GIFFORD • *PORT TROPIQUE* $3.95
NJAMI SIMON • *COFFIN & CO.* $3.95
ERIC KIGHT (RICHARD HALLAS) • *YOU PLAY THE BLACK
AND THE RED COMES UP* $3.95
GERTRUDE STEIN • *BLOOD ON THE DINING ROOM FLOOR* $6.95
KENT NELSON • *THE STRAIGHT MAN* $3.50
JIM NISBET • *THE DAMNED DON'T DIE* $3.95
STEVE FISHER • *I WAKE UP SCREAMING* $4.95
LIONEL WHITE • *THE KILLING* $4.95
JOHN LUTZ • *THE TRUTH OF THE MATTER* $4.95
ROGER SIMON • *DEAD MEET* $4.95
BILL PRONZINI • *MASQUES* $4.95
BILL PRONZINI & BARRY MALZBERG • *THE RUNNING OF BEASTS* $4.95
VICTORIA NICHOLS & SUSAN THOMPSON • *SILK STALKINGS* $12.95
THE BLACK LIZARD ANTHOLOGY OF CRIME FICTION
Edited by EDWARD GORMAN $8.95
THE SECOND BLACK LIZARD ANTHOLOGY OF CRIME FICTION
Edited by EDWARD GORMAN $13.95

Black Lizard Books are available at most bookstores or directly from the publisher. In addition to list price, please sent $1.00/postage for the first book and $.50 for each additional book to Black Lizard Books, 833 Bancroft Way, Berkeley, CA 94710. California residents please include sales tax.